RISING CHAOS

PALDIMORI GODS RISING

BY T.L. CALLAHAN

DRAGON MOUNTAIN
PRESS

First published in United States of America by Dragon Mountain Press
LLC 2020

I

Callahan, T.L. Rising Chaos: Paldimori Gods Rising 3
Copyright © T.L. Callahan 2020
T.L. Callahan asserts their moral right to be identified as the author of this
work.

Library of Congress Control Number: 2019909624

PB ISBN: 978-0-9991225-6-3

EB ISBN: 978-0-9991225-5-6

Edited by: Book Nanny Writing and Editing Services
Cover design by: Covers by Juan
Artwork by: janko_m

This is a work of fiction. Names, characters, places, and incidents either
are the product of the author's imagination or are used fictitiously, and any
resemblance to actual persons, living or dead, business establishments,
events, or locales is entirely coincidental.

Publisher: Dragon Mountain Press LLC, 1250 W. Ohio Pike # 199 Amelia,
OH 45102
Created by Vellum

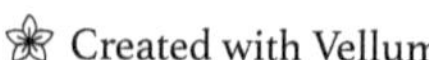 Created with Vellum

ALSO BY BY T.L. CALLAHAN

Paldimori Gods Rising Series

Dawning Chaos

Waking Chaos

Unearthing Gaia

1

"Noooo!" The scream ripped from my throat and was immediately swallowed by the rushing wind as Bennett teleported us away. One moment I was in the horse meadow inside Titan Tower revealing to my best friend Dia King how I had betrayed her. The next, I was standing on a ledge looking down on a city that circled a high mountaintop like an ornate crown. Tall turrets rose into the evening sky, their rooftops alight with glowing balls of fire—the black star-like symbol for the House of Chaos rotating at their center. Below them, white luminescent streets shimmered in the dying light of the evening as people bustled along their cobblestone paths. Fields of bright red flowers grew under a shimmering bubble near the wall on the outskirts of the town. Mountains spread out in the distance as far as the eye could see.

"Damn you, Bennett!" I beat my hands against his shoulders as I slid from his arms to stand on my own wobbly legs. "Teleport us back right now! I have to *explain*. Dia thinks I helped to alter her memories."

"Ask me anything but that, *asteràki*," Bennett said, using

the Greek term for "little star." He grabbed my clenched fists and held them against his chest with one hand. "Lia, I would do anything to keep you safe. Even if I must protect you from yourself. That includes protecting your heart from further abuse."

A haunted look flickered across his face then it disappeared just as quickly. He knocked gently on the closed door on my side of the mental connection we shared as bondmates, and I eased the door open. The sharpest edge of the pain dulled a little as he tugged at my heartache, pulling a bit of it into himself. A shaky breath escaped my lips as the pressure building in my chest lessened. Bennett nudged my chin up, forcing me to meet his gaze. His calloused fingers traced the tears that continued to stream down my cheeks. Those dark brown eyes held mine captive as he silently asked if I wanted him to take all of the pain away. A part of me wanted to let him, but that was a slippery slope leading back to the person I used to be. To the Lia Davies who buried every emotion and never let anyone close. That wasn't who I was trying to be now.

I shook my head.

"Dia made her choice." Bennett's deep voice echoed with a finality that I couldn't accept. My lips parted to say that I could fix this if he would only take me back. That years of friendship couldn't be ended in a single moment. He placed his finger against my lips, stalling my argument. "You must respect that, asteràki, and give her time. Cutting herself off from the friend she considers a sister was a rash decision made out of fear and anger. Dia can no more walk away from you permanently, than you could her. You came back to her once you found a way to move on after the death of your parents. She too must find her own way back to you."

What he said made sense, but it didn't diminish the pain. It didn't silence the pounding need in my veins to find the sister of my heart and make things right between us. I hadn't told Dia when I found out that I was Paldimori: a descendant of the six Primordial Gods of Greek legend. I hadn't told her that she had been there to witness Bennett's step-sister, Natalie—the crazy girl who had tried to kill me repeatedly because of her jealousy over an old boyfriend of mine, and because she was in love with Bennett—attack me at my parents' house. Dia hadn't known, until moments ago, that I had ended up in the hospital because of the injuries from that attack, and not as a result of the fake memories of a boiler explosion that had been planted in her head by one of the Kyrion, the leaders of the six Paldimori Houses. I may not have known about *that* decision until recently, but I had kept secrets from my best friend. It was my fault that she couldn't stand to be near me right now. But what could I do to fix this? My powers were still developing, and my control was crappy at best. Teleporting myself back to the island of Sotirìa where the Paldimori Games took place wasn't going to work, and Bennett was refusing to take me back.

The fight drained out of me, and I slumped against his chest. Bennett wrapped his arms around me. He didn't say anything more, but his embrace was the anchor I needed to hold me together right now. Dia's parting words had stripped my heart bare and squeezed it into a mangled mess. *"I don't want you here anymore. You aren't the person I thought you were. I guess she really did die with her parents."*

All I had ever wanted to do was protect Dia. In the end, I had been the one to hurt her the most. My best friend—the one person who knew me better than anyone else in the world and had stood beside me through it all—was beyond my reach right now. I had thought I knew what was best for her. I had tried to keep her away from all things Paldimori. There was a prophecy that said the Chosen would rise to save the Paldimori race—or doom them to destruction. That had painted a target on my back when I was claimed as a Chosen by the God of Chaos. I had barely survived the attacks during the Games thanks to Natalie and her friends. Now Dia too was a Chosen, claimed by the Goddess Gaia, and in more danger than ever.

Suddenly, a loud howl echoed through the city. Bennett kissed the top of my head and pressed his palms against my back where the House of Chaos symbol was branded into my skin marking me as his bond-mate for life. "Axol knows I am home and has announced my arrival to all of Prometheus. He has become very sensitive to my energy," he said, the fondness for the dog he had rescued clear in his voice. Then he sighed and cupped my cheeks, pulling me away from his chest. His eyes roamed over my face taking in the fatigue that weighed me down—this divide from Dia being only the latest burden thrust on me after weeks of struggling to train my powers and researching the quest I had been tasked with by the Primordial God Chaos—or as he introduced himself to me, Titan Theophanes—to find the twin Houses of the Olympian Omàda.

"I had planned to bring you here to Prometheus to introduce you to our people in a few more weeks," Bennett said. "After I had time to discuss what being a Kyrion means and to teach you the ways of our people." He combed his fingers through his caramel-colored hair, making it stand up in messy spikes. "I have many duties as the leader of the House of Chaos and of all Paldimori people. Duties that you, my bond-mate, will share when you are officially named my co-ruler."

"Wait—What?" If this was his idea of a distraction from

my heartache it was working. Who in their right mind would put me in charge of an entire society of magical people? I couldn't even light a fire with my powers without blowing something up.

"In the eyes of our people, you are a Kyrion-in-training, who will take your place as co-ruler once the official ceremony to announce you has concluded." Bennett watched me closely as if he was waiting for me to lose my shit. *Smart man.* "I told you that when we bonded it was mind, body, and soul. We do not yet understand what it means for you to be Chosen, but you bear my symbol—the symbol of the House of Chaos. You have been my intended co-ruler since the night we sealed our bond and exchanged our wedding vows, even if you did not know at the time what was occurring. That, and gaining control of your powers so that you are not a danger to anyone, is why we have been training so hard. That is also why I have brought you here to my home."

I groaned, dropping my head back onto his muscular chest. "You've got to be fucking kidding me."

2

My bare arms prickled with goose bumps, and my teeth were chattering by the time the winding dirt trail leading down from the mountain gave way to cobblestone streets. Bennett would have teleported us, but I needed the time to compose myself before I met his people.

Across the road from us stood an imposing fortress–mansion hybrid that looked as if someone had cut the two different structures in half and smashed them together. On the left side was a pitted and stained square stone structure reminiscent of some medieval military fortification. The stained-glass windows of its upper floors piqued my inner artist's curiosity about who had commissioned the updates that mashed together such elegance and brutality.

A circular drive led up to the building, wrapping around a familiar-looking large black statue surrounded by glowing hot coals. The statue was of the same man in Bennett's courtyard at Titan Tower—the one that had turned into a naked Titan Theophanes—only here he was half-formed as if rising from the depths of the earth. The starlight that dotted the black stone sparkled in the lights that blazed from the tall windows that lined each floor of the three-story house that made up the right side of Bennett's home. Its walls were of warm, taupe-colored bricks with veins of black running over them as if a toddler had been let loose with a paintbrush. It was like a van Gogh painting: garish and almost crude in its individual components, yet beautiful when viewed as a whole. A four-car attached garage took up the far right side of the driveway. But it was the mountains towering above and surrounding this isolated city and the quaint stone houses lining the streets below that made me wish for a sketch pad. I wrapped my arms around myself to ward off the cold and drew in a deep breath of clean mountain air. *Gods, its beautiful here. I wish Dia could see it. She would—*

The pain hit me again as I remembered that Dia had cut me out of her life. *I'm not giving up on our friendship. Do you hear me, gods? Whatever your plans for us, I won't be leaving her behind again.* We had been through far too much together already. I would do what I needed to do here, and then I was going back to Sotirìa to make things right with my best friend.

A lone woman stood under the lights of the portico at the front entrance of the mansion with Bennett's dog, Axol, at her side. As we started around the circular drive, Axol jumped forward giving an excited yip. Bennett smiled, and I could feel his excitement.

"Go on. I just need to catch my breath," I said, nudging him forward, my chest still heaving from the trek down the mountain. When he didn't budge, I huffed out a panting breath. "Seriously, I'm fine. I know you've missed him these last couple of weeks we've been training. Go see your buddy."

Bennett jogged up the driveway leaving me behind in

the falling light of the evening. Axol darted forward as if he would run to meet Bennett but stopped to look up at the woman by his side. She waved him forward, and the dog shot across the last several feet to his owner. He yipped happily, jumping all around and rubbing up against Bennett's legs. Bennett kneeled down, petting the dog all over, his rarely heard laughter filling the air. My heart warmed as the big dog stood on his hind legs with his paws on Bennett's shoulders in a doggy hug. This was the Bennett very few got to see. The man behind the throne that I had fallen in love with.

I took a few steps up the driveway but then stopped as a thought struck me. The man behind the throne was the one I had gotten to know a bit better, but what about the man who sat on the throne? I was here in the city that he ruled over, and I had no clue about this part of his life. I had seen him as Kyrion Chaos in the Games, and I hadn't liked what I saw. What was his life like here? What would *my* life be like here?

I realized uneasily that our time together at my parents' house had been a reprieve of sorts. It had been our bubble where I was able to convince myself that Bennett and I were a normal couple with this extra sprinkle of extraordinary powers. We hadn't talked about thrones or ruling a hidden society. We hadn't talked about whether we would live in my house or his. There had been training, research, and love-making. Rinse and repeat with conversations about the prophecy and my quest somewhere in the mix. I still didn't know much about this world I had stumbled into—or the man who ruled it all.

Bennett's like a king to the Paldimori. That would make me—

A cold sweat beaded my brow, and I immediately cut the thought off before it could fully take form. *Being a co-ruling*

Kyrion doesn't mean royalty, Lia. You'll probably be like his valet or adviser. I was not cut out to be what equated to royalty in their world. I liked comfy clothes, action movies, and less bullshit in my diet. I rubbed my clammy hands down my thighs trying not to think of all the attention the wedding of Prince Harry and Meghan Markle stirred up. Bennett and I were nothing like that. Right?

I glanced up at that mismatched mansion and had taken two steps backward before I caught myself. "No running," I whispered to myself. "You're stronger than that now."

I forced myself to move forward, focusing on Bennett as my destination. While I had been having a freak-out moment, the woman under the portico had moved closer to where Bennett and Axol were still getting reacquainted. She watched them with her hands clasped in front of her and a radiant smile on her face that quickly died when she noticed me. Golden-brown hair whipped over her shoulders as she turned toward me so fast that I barely saw her move; my arm was wrenched behind my back, and I was forced to the ground. My knees burned where the cobblestones bit through my thin workout pants.

"Who are you? Why are you here?" the woman demanded, twisting my arm further.

"Ouch, shit." I leaned forward trying to ease the ache. "Bennett, we have a problem here. Can you stop with the doggy kisses and get over here?"

Bennett glanced at us and commanded Axol to sit before he came over. "Selene, I would like you to meet Lia. My bond-mate and your soon-to-be Kyrion," he said, barely managing to suppress the laughter in his voice. The woman I assumed was Selene went still behind me. Her grip loosened for a moment before clamping down like a vise on my arm. Why wasn't she letting me go? I struggled, but the woman didn't budge an inch. "You may want to go a bit easy. Lia becomes grouchy when she is in pain or hungry. Also, when I give her orders—or well, most any time. Then things explode."

"*Asshat*," I cursed at him through our connection. "*You would be grouchy too if you were bonded to a bossy know-it-all who makes you work out all the time and hides all of your chocolate.*"

"*It is called practice,*" he corrected, proving my point about being a know-it-all. "*To help you gain control of that exploding part I mentioned and to learn to protect yourself. You should be able to break out of her hold.*" Bennett's amusement was obvious through our bond when he added, "*And your chocolate addiction has turned into an obsession. If there was a chocoholic anonymous program, I would be tempted to enroll you. Although, I do enjoy watching you stomp around the house searching for it. And the inventive names that you call me.*"

I tried again to counter Selene's hold, but it was no use. "*Are you telling her to do this?*" When he only chuckled in return it was all the confirmation I needed. Talk about obsessions: he never missed an opportunity to turn a situation into training. Well, I could play dirty too. I had discovered that my boyfriend loved to collect maps when we had found one in my father's study. "*I'm going to sell that map we found on eBay if you don't get me out of this.*"

The woman released me almost immediately and helped me to my feet. Her voice was smooth as silk and had that same cultured perfection as Bennett's when she said, "Apologies, Lia. I didn't know Bear was bringing a guest." Selene shot Bennett a look that said this was all his fault. "I don't usually keep guests in an armlock. You'll have to fill me in on this new courtship tradition, Bear."

"A bit of training, little rabbit, that is all," Bennett replied with a cocky smirk.

Irritation fizzled in my veins at the cutesy nicknames. "If by 'Bear' you mean the wizard boy here, he isn't great with the details, so I'm not surprised he didn't tell you I was coming," I said with a huff. "*I* didn't even know I was coming here."

It didn't help that Selene looked like a runway model in four-inch heels and a black sleeveless jumpsuit that hugged her slim figure. Her high cheek bones and pouty pink lips were free of any makeup. I, on the other hand, was sweating profusely and my ponytail was hanging halfway off the side of my head. Then there was the fact that the woman had put me on my knees in seconds with heels on and standing on uneven stones. I couldn't even walk in heels on flat ground. I sure as hell hadn't managed to take someone down to their knees, even though we'd been training non-stop.

Her pale arms were deceptively delicate as she held out her hand. The polite smile she gave me was perfunctory without any real emotion. She was like a porcelain doll: perfectly beautiful yet lacking any human emotions. "Selene Roussos, Archai for the House of Chaos."

I shook her hand. "Lia Davies, nice to meet you."

"I apologize for attacking you," Selene motioned to my arm. "I hope I didn't hurt you."

"I'm good," I said, stretching out my arm to relieve the last of the ache. "I blame the Neanderthal you call 'Bear' for our unusual introduction." My elbow landed in Bennett's ribs making him grunt as I pulled the ponytail holder from my hair and finger-combed it into some kind of order. "Unexpected guests would make me jumpy too," I sympathized.

"Yes, I suppose so, given everything that Bear has told

me about you," Selene replied. My glare said he was so dead for talking about me with the runway model. "I'm sure it's been a lot to take in when you are used to the human world." Selene gave me what I think was supposed to be a sympathetic look. "Natalie's childish antics must have painted a horrible picture of our world. I hope you won't judge us all by her actions. Unfortunately, Bear's father over-compensated for the loss of her family by pampering her."

"Sheath your claws, little rabbit," Bennett scolded without much heat, as if this were a topic they argued about often. It was clear these two had a long history together. There was affection there, but I couldn't help wondering if it went beyond that. "Nat has been through a lot. She needs our help."

Selene looked as if she wanted to say more but only nodded. I snorted in disgust. Why was everyone willing to give that psycho Natalie a pass? Did the rest of the Paldimori think like Selene clearly did that I was a whiny newbie from the human world who couldn't deal with some childish bullying?

"I wouldn't call killing me with an arrow through my chest or the various other attempts on my life 'childish antics,'" I gritted out, feeling every bit as grumpy as Bennett claimed me to be. Natalie should have been locked away and stripped of her powers. Instead she got shipped home to daddy with a pat on the head and some bullshit manda-tory therapy sessions. I hated that Bennett forgave his step-sister for kissing him into a catatonic state so easily. Not to mention the boy she had killed or the lives she destroyed—including mine. It was a sore subject that Bennett and I had both avoided to keep the peace.

"Yes, well," Selene waved her hand as if it were no big deal. "Thank the God of Chaos for your healing powers."

Bennett took my hand and placed it on top of his, turning us toward the house before I could argue with Selene. "I believe you had the cooks hold dinner for us?" he asked her.

"Of course. I sent a message on to have another place set for Lia," Selene replied, falling into step beside us. Since I hadn't seen anyone else around, she must have meant she sent them a telepathic message.

"Good." Bennett smiled down at me. "I sent Grayson to get Click for you and to take care of a few things in Sotirìa. I would not expect him until tomorrow."

"I think I'll live without my shadow for a night," I said, grateful the boy who had pledged himself to me was there to watch over the adolescence ink pen I had brought to life. Click could be a handful sometimes. Although the two of them together were likely to give whoever was in charge while Bennett was away a massive headache.

"I'll have another room prepared for him," Selene stated. "Would you like to change first, or should I tell them you're ready for dinner now?"

Bennett turned to me. "I'm starving," I admitted, "and if I get anywhere near a bed I won't be eating tonight."

"We will make our way to the dining hall now. Thank you, Selene."

Selene bowed to him, then walked quickly ahead and through the front door. Bennett wrapped his arms around me before I could follow and pulled my chest flush against his. "There has been so little time for us to truly get to know one another." His lips brushed against my temple, and he sighed as if there was a great weight settling on his shoulders. "These last couple of weeks with you were some of the best days of my life. I do not want to lose sight of us in the midst of all my duties."

I laid my head against his chest and hugged him tightly. Why did it feel as if we were saying goodbye?

"You owe me lots more dates, wizard boy. I'll make sure you keep up your end of the bargain." I looked up into that handsome face noting the shadows that now filled his eyes and the solemn demeanor that was stealing over his features as the heavy mantle of Kyrion settled around him. I resolved in that moment to make sure that there would be more times away from all of this.

I needed to see him smile one more time before we walked into the home of the Kyrion and whatever commitments awaited us there. "Just make sure you wash really good before you bring that mouth anywhere near mine. I think I still see some doggy drool."

I soaked in his smile, memorizing every detail. No matter what happened, we were in this together.

3

I stopped dead in my tracks as we stepped through the entrance door to Bennett's home. A stone bridge stretched from the entrance doors across a wide bed of hot coals to an open archway with a grand staircase beyond. Benches were placed every few feet apart near the edges of the wide bridge. Statues of the six Paldimori gods stood, three to a side, in recesses along the walls. Overhead, tendrils of flames of various sizes floated near the vaulted ceiling like the *aurora borealis*.

"Uh, did we just enter a really weird sauna?" The heat was almost too much after the freezing cold outside.

"Each House has an affinity with something that they incorporate into their homes. It was once a law for all Paldimori to live as closely entwined with their affinity power as possible. Ours is fire," Bennett answered and used his telekinesis to float a hot coal into the palm of his hand. "The stronger the power, the more immunity to fire descendants of the House of Chaos are gifted with. Thermal energy —heat—is the catalyst for fire. We are naturally drawn to it for the strength it bolsters in our powers. Children are gifted a hot coal at the age of two as a sort of primer to begin working their fire powers." Bennett tumbled the hot coal around in his hand as if it was a worry stone. "The heat is also soothing to us. You will find that most homes here have a fireplace, at least, or hot-coal bed. This entranceway was my mother's design. She wanted our people to feel welcome and comfortable in her home. To father's great annoyance she would often settle grievances here rather than in the formal throne room."

Wow! Hot coals were like power-boosting security blankets to these people. Shopping for Christmas presents here was going to be a breeze. Wait, did they even celebrate Christmas? If not, that was going on my list of changes to make.

Bennett tossed the coal back into the pit below as two men approached us. They each wore sleek uniforms covered in black scales from the high collar to the tops of their black boots. Black swords were strapped to their waists. Black metal star-like symbols of the House of Chaos ran down the back of each arm looking like throwing stars. They bowed low to Bennett. Then to me. The heat that stung my cheeks wasn't only from the hot coals. Having people bow to me was a brand-new experience and not one I could ever see myself being comfortable with.

"Talos Moore. Talos Gavril." Bennett greeted them with a swooping hand motion and the men rose from their bowed positions. "It is good to see you. The Archai has kept me appraised of the tower attacks. However, I would like to hear your own impressions. Come to the control room tomorrow morning and bring any others that have been to the towers."

"It will be done, Kyrion Bennett," the men answered in unison, their respect for their leader plain to see. The man on the left said, "It's good to have you home, sir. And we welcome you, my lady."

"Thank you," I said, shifting uneasily at the "my lady" part. I had grown used to Grayson saying those words, but it was almost like a form of affection from him. These men had only just met me.

"It is good to be home, Talos Gavril." Bennett's tone was polite yet distant. It was as if all emotion had bled from him the moment we stepped through the door. "You may return to your posts now and if there are any more attacks report them at once."

The men bowed again and walked out the door.

"Why are they 'my ladying' me? And why do your people name everything the same?" I asked thinking of every leader passing on the name Kyrion Chaos and how confusing that might get. "Although, I could see where naming every guy 'Talos' would be easier than picking up a baby-name book all the way out here on mount-nowhere. I'm not sure even Amazon could find this place."

The shadows lifted a bit from Bennett's eyes as he swept an errant strand of hair from my cheek. "They are showing respect for your position as my intended bond-mate," Bennett said. "And Talos is not their name, but their title. The guides for each House—some of whom you met at the Games—are similar to your Secret Service. Their job is to protect the Kyrion and other crucial members of our society, such as the contestants in the Games—" A shiver raced down my spine when he mentioned the Games, and everything that had happened to me there flashed through my mind. There had been too many near-death experiences for me in the Games to ever think fondly of Sotirìa, no matter how amazing the island was. I pushed the memories aside before they could overwhelm me and trigger my powers. "—the Talosi protect the House bases."

It took me a moment to understand what he'd been saying. "Guides are like bodyguards and the Talosi are like your army, right?"

"Yes, asteràki. One more lesson for tonight, then we eat." Bennett flattened his hand with the palm facing down and held it out toward me. Then placed my hand on top of his. "This is the way unrelated men and woman who have reached bonding age are permitted to touch. Until we go through the Bonding Ceremony, this is how I will escort you."

"Of course, there's another ceremony," I said. "Should I not show my ankles either for fear of sending men into a lustful frenzy?" Considering what we had been doing on every flat surface of my parents' house, this was ridiculous. Weren't we already "married" according to their traditions? "You may need to adjust your teleporting compass because I think we went back in time." My sarcasm made the corner of Bennett's lips twitch. "I'm almost afraid to ask, but why is there a bonding age limit?"

"The age limit is now sixteen and is in place to protect our youth. Mother wanted young men and women to have a chance to enjoy their childhoods free from the courting traditions. Arranged bondings at the time of birth—like my mother's—were very popular in the past. Father was seven at the time and the most powerful suitor." There was a mixture of sadness and anger in his voice. Bennett's hand tensed beneath mine before he forced himself to relax once more.

"Thankfully, Mother changed the laws, or I would have been bonded long before we met. We may bond with anyone but finding a true bond-mate—the one person the

God of Chaos intended to be the other part of our soul—is difficult. For many, it will never happen." Bennett brushed the back of his fingers down my cheek, and I finally understood how special our bond was. No wonder he was fiercely protective of me and so damn insistent that I learn to protect myself. "Arranged bondings are still popular in families that want to produce more powerful children, but the couple must consent to it now."

"How progressive of you guys to allow people to say no to their parents' pick on who they'll spend the rest of their lives with." My sarcasm was sharp enough to cut. "And don't get me started on the pairing up people to 'produce more powerful children,'" I mockingly air quoted in a manly sounding voice. "That's some doctor Frankenstein kinda messed up. Seriously, Bennett, how far back in time did we travel?"

"Change is slow to come to our world, Lia. My mother was the most progressive Kyrion we have had, and she faced a lot of opposition from our people and my father." He sighed and gripped my shoulders. "I did not say that I approved of those things, but I cannot change thousands of years of tradition overnight."

"Sorry. I know you're doing your best." I hugged him tight, then pulled back to give him a teasing smile. "I make no promises on keeping my opinion to myself, but I'll at least try to not to burn bras in protest."

My stomach picked that moment to give a loud rumble. Bennett's lips lifted in a semi-smile that gave me hope that he wasn't lost to the role of Kyrion completely—at least with me. "Come. We are keeping you from dinner, and I would hate for the servant's first impressions of their future Kyrion to be a hangry Lia."

I wanted to tell him he was being a butthead, but it was

the truth. My stomach sounded like I was ready to eat someone, and my temper would match if I didn't get food soon.

The intense heat of the entranceway diminished as soon as we stepped through the archway on the other side of the room. I gawked in awe as we passed the grand staircase that branched off twice to second and third floor balconies. We turned right down a sconce-lined hallway with the occasional painting hanging on the walls. One of the largest was a family portrait. The woman was beautiful with light brown hair and pale brown eyes. She smiled with the glow of new motherhood as she glanced down into the face of the baby in her arms. At her shoulder stood a stern-looking man staring straight ahead. His dark brown eyes seemed to bore into me, leaching the lingering heat from my bones. I couldn't put my finger on it, but I could swear I knew him from somewhere.

"I don't think they've been apart this long since the Kyrion brought him home," Selene was saying as we approached an open doorway. "It was good to see the Kyrion happy."

"The pup has missed him," an elderly woman replied as we entered the room. The woman standing next to Selene had white hair trapped in a bun on top of her head and wore the typical long black dress of the women servants. They stood on the left side of the room at the end of a long rectangular table covered in a cream tablecloth. Light from lantern-shaped sconces that lined the walls and hung from the ceiling reflected off metal dishes of various sizes spread across the end of the table. The elderly woman leaned over to lift the lid of one of the dishes and gave the steaming soup a stir. "It's unlike the Kyrion to not take Axol—"

"Ann, something smells divine," Bennett called out, interrupting the elderly woman. Selene had noticed us right away but hadn't clued the other woman in on our presence. It was almost as if she wanted us to overhear that conversation. Selene ignored my questioning look her way and nodded approvingly toward our stacked hands as we neared the table. I wiped the assessing look from my face when Bennett glanced at me with a quick reassuring tilt of his lips.

Bennett may have brushed it off, but the women's conversation bothered me. I hadn't thought about why Axol might not have come with us to stay at my parents' house. Training and combing through my father's study for more clues that might help me find a starting place for my quest had consumed my time. Now I felt like an ass for being the high-maintenance girlfriend who needed her man to be by her side constantly, keeping him away from his friends. My eyes narrowed on Selene. Had she been trying to make a point to let me know that Bennett had left Axol behind because of me?

Ann dipped into a deep bow that I wouldn't have thought possible for her age. "Dinner is served, Kyrion Bennett. I've made both your favorites." Bennett moved to help her rise, and they spoke quietly, the affection between them was clear even though their interaction was all very formal. My stomach rumbled again, and I turned away to give them their privacy. I walked alongside the long rectangular table lifting the heavy metal lids. There was a roast, mashed potatoes, candied yams, corn, some type of bisque, apple pie, lemon tarts, and more. I snatched a lemon tart and popped it in my mouth. The tangy-sweet taste hit my palette, and I groaned in pleasure. A gasp sounded, and I looked up.

My cheeks, full of pastry, heated beneath three pairs of eyes staring at me. Bennett was wearing his Kyrion face, but I was starting to pick up little tells. The light in his eyes said he was amused, but the set of his mouth said I had fucked up. Ann was much easier to read: she was shocked and outraged. I swallowed down the tart, and it hit my stomach like a rock as my nerves jittered wondering what I had done wrong.

"The blessing must be said before a meal. None eat before the Kyrion is served and has taken the first bite," Selene advised, with a barb in her tone that said I had committed an unforgivable sin. Those golden eyes flared with something that looked a lot like contempt before the emotionless wall went back up. The moment had been so quick that I wondered if maybe I had imagined it. I was tired and hungry, after all. I wouldn't admit it to Bennett, but that was definitely a combination that brought out my grouch.

Selene got that faraway look as if she were speaking tele-pathically, and I had an idea who she was talking to. I eased open the door on my side of our connection just enough to hear what she was saying. *"Bear, are you sure?"*

Bennett appraised me as if searching for something, fully aware that I was eavesdropping. There was a tickle along our connection as his mind brushed briefly against mine. *"Yes, the Desmòs—the true bond blessed by the gods—has formed. I feel Lia in my soul, her presence is like the sun lighting up my days. She is my true bond-mate,"* he responded, his eyes soft and filled with love as he watched me. If there had been anything more than friendship between them in the past, he had made it clear who he was with now. It took everything I had not to throw myself into his arms and kiss him sense-less. He smirked. *"There will be time for that later when I get you alone, asteràki."*

Selene's voice was unexpectedly soft as she said, *"I am happy for you, my friend. May the gods bless your union."* Then her emotions were wiped away as if it was a momentary lapse as she continued, "*The guides and Talosi have already been told that she is your intended bond-mate. It will be best to appear to uphold the traditions and let all of our people think you are not yet bonded. I'll make the Bonding Ceremony arrangements two days from now. With those kinds of looks being shared between you, I doubt this ruse would last any longer than that.*"

Bennett's chuckle filled my head as he answered her. "*You are always so practical, little rabbit. And always right.*" His humor died away to be replaced by a nostalgic sigh. "*I miss the days of your enthusiastic bouncing about and asking a million questions. I have learned many things from my bonding, but mostly that my mother was right: there is more to life than duties. I hope you realize that for yourself someday, my friend.*"

"*You and my position are all I have left,*" Selene stated firmly. "*It is enough,*" she added and turned towards the servant. "*Now introduce your wife to Ann, and let's eat. My lemon tarts are waiting.*"

I wondered what had happened to Selene, but I would never ask. Her story was her own to tell, and I felt guilty for overhearing what she had thought was a private conversation. She and I had this one thing in common, though. I knew all too well about burying your past and locking your emotions away. Hopefully one day she would find her way back from that lonely existence too.

Bennett came to me and placed my hand over his once more before escorting me over to join the women. "This is Jillian Nova Davies, my intended bond-mate," he said introducing me to Ann. The older woman gasped, her weathered hand coming up to press to her wrinkled lips as her eyes filled with tears. "She was raised in the human world and is still learning our customs."

Ann bowed deeply again. "My lady, I'm so pleased to meet you." She beamed a wrinkled smile at Bennett. "In all the years I have served your family I never thought I would see this day. I only wish that your mother was here to see this." A heavy sadness filled the room for a moment as they all seemed lost in their own memories. Then Ann clapped her hands, breaking the pall. "Today is a day of celebration. I'm sorry, my lady, if I had known you were coming, I could have made something special for you as well."

"I'm sure I'll enjoy whatever's available," I said hesitantly unsure now that I'd already made a fool of myself once. My stomach tightened with nerves. I tried to joke my way out of the awkwardness. "You can blame Mr. Short-on-Details for my last-minute addition. Next time you should tell us to fix our own dinner if we're going to be so late."

The slight compression of Selene's lips was the only outward sign of her displeasure, but I felt the weight of it curl around me as if her emotions were an intangible force. Ann sputtered in shock before she recovered herself and gave me a strained smile. "I would never leave a Kyrion to make their own meals, my lady. It is my privilege to cook for you both."

"I thank you for staying late, Ann," Bennett said, before I could apologize for my blunder. "Though, you should have left this to the others. Take tomorrow to rest." Ann tried to protest, but he pulled on his commanding Kyrion voice. "The kitchens will run without you for a day. You will rest tomorrow, that is an order."

"Yes, Kyrion Bennett. I will send the others out to see to the meal," Ann replied with another bow before disappearing through a door along the opposite wall from where we had entered.

Bennett led me around the table to the first chair and left me standing there before moving to the chair at the head of the table. Selene took up position behind the chair directly across from me. A man and two women servants in all black entered the room from the door Ann had exited through earlier. The male servant pulled out Bennett's chair, helping him to sit. Then the women, in turn, helped me and, finally, Selene.

I started to reach for the water glass, but Selene's pointed look stilled my hand. I waited awkwardly while the female servants loaded plates again in the same order. This was all wrong. Any minute now I expected to be told women were to remain silent and subservient. That wasn't me. I was opinionated and, even if I didn't like the spotlight, I was used to making my own decisions. I had owned my own art gallery back in Port Lawson, for god's sakes, and now I was being treated like an invalid.

Bennett raised a black goblet, and Selene copied him. I picked mine up too, thinking we were going to do a toast; instead, the two of them began speaking in unison. "God of Chaos, hear my plea. Bless my House and this bounty you have given me. Save my soul for the skies, and keep my Kyrion ever wise. Rise gods once more and let my powers through you pour." Then they shouted, "*Anerrhiphtho kybos!*" This must have been the prayer that the guides had said at the meal where I met the other Potentials during the Games. The one where Nikki, aka Busty Bigmouth, had been talking too much for me to hear it at the time.

The bizarre meal continued as Bennett took a bite of his potatoes, and we were free to eat. Selene carefully selected one of the lemon tarts from the pile that covered half of her plate and took a dainty bite making me feel like a complete slob for having shoved the entire thing into my mouth earlier. I poked at the roast, my mouth watering, but my stomach still heavy with nerves. This was like meeting your boyfriend's parents for the first time and knowing that they found you unworthy of their son.

"What did that mean?" I asked to break the heavy silence. "That thing that you shouted at the end of your prayer."

"It is an old Greek motto that translates as 'let the die be cast,'" Bennett explained, swirling the wine in his goblet before raising it toward the wall across from me. I had been so caught up in my bungled first introductions that I hadn't noticed the mural covering the wall on either side of the doorway where we had entered. The vivid strokes of the painting were amazing, and I would be across the room in a heartbeat studying every line if I wasn't worried about breaking another rule.

A dark man-shaped figure floated in a starry sky. Galaxies spun in his eyes, and he seemed to be pulling from the very fabric of space to weave together streams of power. The six gods and goddesses I was becoming familiar with floated around him. The color of their powers danced around the dark sky-god's fingers and surrounded their six robed forms. All around them strange worlds, people, and creatures were being created or destroyed. "It is our way of acknowledging that we all play the games of gods. My people were once gifted with visions that showed us the possibilities that are fated, each thread tied to a pivotal choice. But as our powers have faded, the gift of visions was lost to us. Now each day is a gamble and our fates dark to us."

"I don't believe that," I said, setting my fork aside. "You said yourself there's choice involved. I have to believe that people can change their lives, or I wouldn't be here."

Bennett held up a hand to stop Selene when she would have said something. "She does not know our laws.

That is why I have brought her here. You must teach her, Selene."

"Bennett," Selene said in a hard voice that communicated her reluctance, "she insulted your hospitality twice this evening and basically spouted blasphemy just now. How do you expect me to teach all that we have learned over a lifetime in a matter of weeks?"

"I did not say it would be easy, little rabbit." Bennett's hand covered hers where it was pressed hard against the table. "I said only that you are the person fit for the job. You know all of the recorded history in our library, and my mother trained you alongside me. You know how to be Kyrion as well as I do." Selene's shoulders pulled back in pride at his praise. "You are nearly as strong in power as Kafàli Harris. If not for our laws and my father's insistence, you would have been leader of the guides. But it is you—my Archai, my adviser—that I trust to run this House in my absence. It is only you I would entrust with this task. Will you teach Lia, my friend?"

Something flickered in Selene's golden eyes too quickly to name as she stared at Bennett. The moment drew out, tension charging the air as we waited for her decision. Jealously clawed at my chest, and my hands trembled to pull my boyfriend away from her. *Keep it together, Lia. Selene isn't trying to steal your boyfriend. She's his childhood friend. Besides weren't you just giving yourself a pep talk about not monopolizing him?*

Selene turned to me, her voice quiet yet fierce. "We are a race far older than your humans. You might consider us old-fashioned, even barbaric. But this is our way of life, and these are now your people. We have pride and great respect for our Kyrion." The love for her people and Bennett was obvious in every passionate word. And she was right. Who was I to judge them? I was the newcomer here, and I would have to earn my place amongst them.

"Lia, will you swear to respect our traditions? To follow everything I tell you, and take your studies seriously?"

My legs shook under the table, and I pressed my hands to my knees to stop them. The inborn need to run from this commitment was strong, but I was stronger. I was only now starting to realize my inner strength and to find my true self. Would letting them mold me into a Kyrion take me further from that goal or closer?

I wasn't perfectly poised, graceful, or diplomatic like Selene. I was awkward and uncomfortable with their social hierarchy. My temper and my mouth could take on a mind of their own. Yet, I was marked as a member of the House of Chaos and was bonded to its leader. Bennett was tied to this world in so many ways that if I rejected this, then I could lose him too.

"I can't guarantee that I won't get mad or try to change things if I think they're wrong." Then I said the words that would take me down a path I never anticipated, "But I promise to try my best to become Kyrion here."

"I'll take it," Selene replied with a hint of respect for my honesty. "We are agreed. Your lessons will start tomorrow morning at dawn in the throne room."

"At dawn?" I asked, already dreading the morning. I wasn't a bed slug like Dia but that was early even for me. I ignored the pang that thinking of Dia caused. Maybe my time here would help me work through the heartache and come up with a solution.

Bennett gave Selene's hand a squeeze, then let it go. "Thank you, my friend."

Selene picked up her wine and drank it down. "Don't thank me yet. We only have two weeks to make Lia ready."

We all winced as my fork screeched across the plate completely missing the piece of roast I was aiming for. "Two weeks? That isn't enough time. I was thinking maybe a few years."

"Only Selene knows we are already fully bonded," Bennett said casually, stirring his soup. Dark brown eyes met mine and for a moment there was sympathy there. And something darker that sent a jolt of unease through me. Then the mask of the Kyrion fell over them, cutting off all emotion. "Word of your identity will not remain secret for long. I cannot make excuses to keep our people from meeting you. The Bonding Ceremony will take place two days from now and the Coronation Ceremony in two weeks. That is all the time I can give you."

"What if I'm not ready by then?"

It was Selene that responded. "Here with only the three of us there is a kind of safety. But if you publicly break our laws, Bennett will have no choice but to punish you."

There went my appetite again.

4

"Creations change."

"No!" I screamed into the humid air of the Emerald Rainforest at Titan Tower.

The voice sounded again. That cold, emotionless voice that had invaded my body the night I touched the statue in Bennett's courtyard. *"Life is change. Change is life."*

Not Dia. Please, not Dia. You bastard gods, leave her alone!

Roots speared into Dia's wrists, and she started screaming. I stood ready to battle the gods themselves to spare her this pain. Just as I darted forward Bennett grabbed me about the waist, lifting me off my feet as I kicked and fought to reach her.

"This is the way it has to be, Lia," Bennett said with a grunt as I landed a kick to his shin. "The Goddess Gaia will not be denied. You help no one by trying to interfere. You cannot fight a god. You must let Dia be claimed."

"You don't know what it's like," I cried out, desperate to make him understand and let me go to Dia. "To be claimed by a god like that. You've always had your powers and known who you are. Dia and I have been living a lie this whole time. Then some all-powerful gods shove their hand up our asses and make us dance to their tune like puppets. None of you have any idea what it means that we're Chosen or what will happen. Don't you dare tell me to sit back and accept this."

The wind surged around us rustling the trees. A burning sensation filled my veins and started to build in intensity. My gaze locked on the spot where my best friend hovered in the air, her blood raining down to soak into the ground. Helplessness hollowed out my insides. My struggles ceased, and I slumped against Bennett's hard body. Acid poured into me, the pain pushing out everything else until I dropped to my knees panting. Bennett kneeled in front of me shouting in concern, but the pain dug its claws into me and would not let go. It filled me to overflowing. Then burst out in an explosion of fire.

The ground trembled. I floated into the air. Anger, fear, and pain were all I knew. They consumed me as white light poured from my eyes. Somehow Bennett reached me and wrapped himself around me. He blasted through the door to our connection, "Forgive me. You must control the power, or you will kill us all."

I bolted upright in bed, clutching my stomach where I could still feel the phantom sensation of Bennett siphoning off my powers that day that Dia had been claimed. I dropped my sweaty forehead into my palms and took a shaky breath. Fear and anger clung to me, making my head pound.

God no, not again.

When Dia had been claimed, my own powers had gotten a boost. Where once it had taken great concentration to locate the powers inside me, now they glowed at my center like an iridescent ball of irritated fireflies. And my emotions seemed to be feeding the frenzy. The fireflies took flight swarming through my body to leave trails of fire in their wake, and my breathing hitched. It felt as if that fire was pulling all of the oxygen from this huge bedroom where a servant had deposited me last night—alone.

I flung off the white comforter with embroidered silken poppies and rolled to the right side of the king-sized bed. Reflected in the tall gold-trimmed mirror which took up a large portion of the wall opposite me was a painting of a beautiful woman in a formal gown which hung over the bed. I looked out of place, reflected there next to her in this elegant room in my T-shirt, Snatch Dragon underwear, and messy bed-head.

My chest heaved as I struggled to hold onto the power, but it was no use. Fire lit up my palms and climbed my arms. I had learned, after a few accidents at my parents' house, that a cold shower worked really well when this happened. Leaping from the bed, I raced across the wooden floors toward the bathroom, hoping I would make it in time.

Unfortunately, I wasn't familiar with this new room in Bennett's home and tripped over the edge of a rug sending a wave of fire surging out of me. The antique-looking red brocade couch and chairs in the sitting area near the fire-place burst into flames. The golden-hued rug also covered in red poppies disintegrated into ash around my prone body leaving only the outer edges untouched.

"*Lia!*" Bennett called through our connection, having no doubt felt my panic. He appeared beside me seconds later and pulled me to my feet. "Are you hurt?"

"I'm fine, just turned into a human torch again," I replied sarcastically, squinting as Bennett used his telekinesis to turn on the lights, brushing his hands over my arms as he searched for injuries. "I'm pretty sure I killed your fancy furniture," I grumbled, looking at the charred remains. "This is why we can't have nice things."

Bennett glanced briefly at the destruction but didn't bat an eye. It wasn't like I hadn't set things on fire before, although, it wasn't usually this bad. It was going to take me hours to clean up this mess. His gaze swept the rest of the room and paused on the painting. A confused look crossed his face before he turned back to me. Bennett flicked ash from my hair, his lips twitching as he tried not to laugh. "I thought as my wife you might want to redecorate anyway."

"Sure, laugh it up, wizard boy," I teased, shooting a feigned glare his way. "We can't all be magical prodigies like you." I wiped an ash-coated finger down his cheek leaving a trail of soot behind to break up all of that masculine perfection. The muscles in his bare chest flexed beneath my gritty touch as my hands wandered lower of their own accord. The man was a sinful temptation, in or out of clothes. It boggled my mind every time I realized he was all mine. "And it's *girlfriend*, not wife."

Bennett had tricked me into marrying him in the ways of the Paldimori because he had wanted access to my powers to help defend his people from their enemies. At least, at first, that was his reasoning, but somewhere along the way we fell in love, and everything changed. He still had a lot to make up for, though. Our agreement was that we would try dating to get to know each other better before I would acknowledge myself as his wife and put the ring that now hung around my neck back on my finger. But secretly I got a little thrill every time he called me his wife. As much as I loved poking at that infamous control of his, I was starting to wonder why I was still protesting against something I wanted just as badly as he did: to let the world know that we belonged to each other

"You will get there with time, asteràki." Bennett sucked in a breath when my touch slid over his hard abs, and he grabbed my hands to keep them from traveling lower. "You need to practice with your powers more."

"We've been training non-stop." An exasperated breath puffed out of me sending more ash falling to the floor. I pulled away and started rolling up the carpet. "I'm tired of being isolated from everyone." I stopped rolling and sat back on my knees as I looked at him over my shoulder. "Not that you and Grayson haven't been great about trying to help with my control, but I can't stay locked away here in Prometheus forever." Bennett and Grayson were like security blankets that helped me control the powers when they were around, so I wasn't a danger to others. But I had missed Dia horribly while training. What was I going to do now that she had booted me out of her life completely? And how was I going to tiptoe my way around the people in Bennett's house without blowing someone up? Heartache and worry filled me, and my powers stirred again. I quickly went back to trying to clean up the mess to distract myself.

Bennett gripped my arm and pulled me to my feet once more. "Leave that for the servants."

"Are you serious? Look what I did," I said, sweeping my hand out to indicate the destroyed sitting area. "This is worse than anything I've torched before. If I'm going to be a walking time-bomb the least I can do is clean up whatever I destroy. And can't we call them something besides servants? It makes me think of slaves and has me itching to stage a revolt."

"Leave this. They *serve*, that is why they are called servants. If you revolted, you would do so alone. It is an honor for them to fulfill their duty," Bennett declared, refusing to let go of me so I could go back to cleaning. I frowned at him wanting to argue, but his finger gently traced the dark circles that lived permanently under my eyes these days. "You are tired and worried. Your sleep has either been interrupted with bad dreams or you have been too restless to go to bed. Most nights when we stayed at your parents' house, I found you dozing in the library surrounded by piles of books." His hands landed on my shoulders, kneading my tight muscles. "You cannot keep pushing yourself this way."

"I know. It's just that I feel this sense of urgency." Even thinking about all the questions left unanswered had my chest clenching with anxiety. Time was running out. The Paldimori Games had to be completed within the calendar year, which only left a few months. Dia and the other contestants would be completing the second competition in a few days, but there were still four more to go. Somehow, I knew that this quest I had been tasked with was tied to that timeline as well. "Titan said I was the one who had to find the twin Houses. If I don't figure this out, something bad is going to happen. Don't ask me how I know that. I just do."

"*We*, my stubborn wife. *We* must figure this out." Bennett pulled me into his arms. "Do you not remember when I told you that I signed up for the whole package as long as I got you? I love you, asteràki. You are not alone."

"I love you too, my wizard." I wrapped my arms around his neck and pulled his lips to mine. The kiss was soft and sweet, but quickly turned scorching. Bennett pulled me flush against his body. His hardness pressed into me, and heat pooled between my thighs. I broke away from those sinful lips. "Ok, you've convinced me," I panted. "There may be certain benefits to us working together. How about you use your wizarding powers to magic all the books onto

Google. Then your *girlfriend* can use her mad internet skills to find all the answers."

"I thought you might see things my way." Bennett's fingers pushed under my T-shirt to caress the lines of the symbol on my back. "Our knowledge cannot be shared with the human world no matter how much more convenient it might be to have them on your internet. And my *wife* has other skills that I am in need of just now."

My pulse jumped as those clever fingers of his traced the seam of my underwear until they settled against the damp spot that was forming. "I-I need ..."

"What do you need, Lia?" His finger pressed against my throbbing clit, eliciting a moan. "This, or perhaps something deeper ... thicker. Tell me what you need, and it is yours."

"Bennett ..." My powers were starting to grow once more.

"Open," he demanded as he mentally nudged against the closed door and shoved my legs apart at the same time. I eased open the door on my side of our connection. He tugged at my powers, eliciting a groan that was part relief and part arousal as he twined them with his to keep me from going supernova. My clothes disappeared, and his rough fingers sank into me. I cried out in shocked pleasure as he teleported us directly into the shower. Cool water poured over my feverish skin turning gray as the ash was washed away. Bennett's fingers drove into me again. My back hit the tiled wall taking what was left of my breath away.

"What do you need, asteràki? I will not ask again."

"You!" I shouted as his fingers found that perfect spot inside me that drove me crazy. "I need you."

"Where do you need me? Here?" His teeth tugged at my bottom lip before he took my mouth in a hard kiss. He abruptly broke away and bent his head to suck sharply on my left nipple. His deep voice invaded my head, "*Is it here that you need me?*"

"Oh god. Please," I whispered, hovering right on the edge of bliss. "Damn you, Bennett, I need you inside me. Now."

A wave of energy plastered me to the wall. My hands were pinned. My legs spread wide as Bennett used our combined powers to lift me up into the air. His eyes captured mine as he dropped me onto his hard length, wringing a cry from my lips at the sudden fullness. The blue ring surrounding his irises pulsed in time with the synchronized rhythm of our hearts. His hips bucked setting a hard pace, and my orgasm tore through me.

"Mine," Bennett said gruffly as his palms pressed into mine and the warmth of his release spilled inside me.

"Body and soul," I gasped, recalling the words from the bonding ritual. Bennett released me from the wall, and I wrapped myself around him in a full body hug. "And you're mine too, wizard boy."

5

Sunlight streamed through the tall windows of my bedroom rousing me from the best sleep I'd had in a while. I stretched languidly across the plush bed, smiling at the delicious aches all over my body. We had made love several times late into the night and fallen into an exhausted sleep in my bed. I smiled wickedly. *Take that, Selene. Bennett broke one your stuffy old rules to be with me.*

Selene and Bennett had stayed behind last night after dinner to discuss whatever it is that advisers had to tell their Kyrion at nearly midnight. I had been informed that the Kyrion used separate suites, and I wasn't to stay with Bennett until after the coronation. I was sent off to my bedroom with a servant feeling jealous and irritated. Luckily Bennett's visit had worked most of that out. I turned over ready to reward him for being the rebel, but his side of the bed was empty.

Disappointment slapped me in the face. Of course, he wouldn't want anyone to know he had broken one of their rules. Our night together now seemed like some tawdry affair to be hidden and my happy buzz plummeted to its death.

I pressed the comforter to my naked chest as I sat up in bed, the movement reflected in the mirror drawing my attention. My disheveled appearance was a jarring disparity amongst the elegance of the room. The poised lady in the painting over the bed seemed to mock me with her perfect cream-colored ballgown dotted with red poppies and her pale blonde hair swept up into a flawless twist. Her red lips were parted in a bright smile but there was something about her eyes that seemed sad.

A chill brushed cross my bare shoulders as a whisper fluttered by my ear. *"Leave."*

I bolted from the bed, still clutching the comforter as I searched the room but there was no one around. I let out the breath I had been holding and shook my head at my foolishness. A red robe laying across the padded bench at the end of the bed caught my eye. That hadn't been here last night and neither had the wooden trunk that sat beside it. I tossed the comforter onto the bed and slipped into the warm robe. My fingers traced over the familiar carvings of poppies on the lid of the wooden trunk. This was the trunk that had been left in the bedroom of my condo after I had gotten out of jail for the fake money and photos Natalie had planted at my home. With everything going on, I had completely forgotten about it. How had it gotten here?

I opened the lid to find clothes in my size and my favorite toiletries, just like before. Finally, I could get out of that torturous spandex they called workout gear and into my comfy clothes. I pulled on a pair of jeans, my favorite Princess Leia T-shirt, and tennis shoes.

The items on the bench weren't the only new things in my room. Someone had cleaned up the charred mess from last night and put two red-and-gold striped sofas in the space. A round table stood near the fireplace with a breakfast tray sitting in front of one of the two high-backed chairs embroidered with red poppies.

"Good morning, my lady," came a cheerful woman's voice. "Kyrion Bennett arranged for breakfast to be brought to your room. Let me know if it's cold, I'll run it back to the kitchen for something fresh."

A middle-aged woman with hair such a dark brown it was almost black and kind hazel eyes stood in front of the gold curtains covering the other half of the wall beside the giant mirror. She wore the same long black chiffon dress as the other servants I had seen.

"Where did you come from? I didn't hear the door."

"Oh no, I was in the closet putting your things away," the lady hitched her thumb toward the gold curtain over her shoulder. "I've been here cleaning and getting you settled in as the Archai requested." She walked toward me and lifted the lid on the breakfast tray. "Here let me serve your breakfast."

"No, no. It's fine." I waved her away. "I can serve myself. Uh, what's your name?"

"My name is Lydia, my lady," she said as the smile slipped from her lips and she nervously wrung her hands. "If you're not pleased with my service, I can send someone else?"

"Uh, no that isn't— Sure you can serve me."

I'd never hurt someone's feelings over *not* letting them do work before. I felt awkward as hell as Lydia pulled out my chair and placed a napkin in my lap. She beamed a smile as if I had given her the best present ever. I pointed out which foods I wanted, and she put them on my plate. I worried that she would try to chew my food for me next, but she moved off to straighten something on the fireplace mantle.

"Selene has had the seamstresses working since first light on your gowns." Lydia chatted away as I tried to eat under her watchful eye. "I can't wait to see them. Oh, and the runners have brought back some lovely things too." She rattled on about all the dresses I had to choose from for dinners, House meetings, and audiences, but I had stopped listening.

"Time-out," I held up my hands in a T-shape stopping her before she could go on. "What are runners and why am I hearing the word 'dresses' so much?"

"Kyrion Calidora always wore dresses, my lady," Lydia replied cautiously. "We didn't know that Kyrion Bennett had found his intended bond-mate or the seamstresses would have had your wardrobe completed for your arrival." Well, that confirmed it. The cat was out of the bag about who I was already. It seemed that the Paldimori weren't that different from humans when it came to gossip. Lydia continued, "Selene sent the runners out—they're the servants who get what we need from the outside world. You have a fine selection of daily dresses to choose from. The seamstresses vow, my lady, they will have your formal gowns ready for the ceremonies."

"Lydia, relax. I'm fine with whatever the runners brought. I could just pick something out from what's already here for the ceremonies; there's no need for the seamstresses to make me anything," I said trying to reassure her. It bothered me the way she hung on my every reaction so nervously, like my opinion was life or death. Would Bennett allow his people to be punished over something as stupid as not having clothes prepared for them? "I prefer jeans or any kind of pants—well, except spandex—over dresses."

"But, my lady, it's tradition to have formal gowns for the ceremonies. And Kyrion Calidora—"

"The dress lover. Yes, I know but I'm not her." Lydia paled as if I had said I would be going to these ceremonies naked. I felt like I was walking blind through a field of land-mines, and I kept stepping on them. How in the hell was I going to learn to be a Kyrion?

Son of a bitch, I was supposed to have met Selene hours ago!

I gulped down my orange juice and stacked the bacon on a napkin to take with me. "I'll take a look at the clothes as soon as I'm done with my lessons. I've gotta go!"

"But, my lady—" Lydia called out, pointing toward clothes she had just laid out on the padded bench, and stared in horror as I speed-walked to the red double doors and waved goodbye before quickly exiting the suite.

I turned down the wide hallway passing by a similar set of black doors that led to Bennett's suite. The plain cream-colored walls of the hallway were soothing after all the red and gold in my room. Every so often there were gold tables with black vases of red poppies that I didn't remember seeing last night. Another servant—maybe around the age of nineteen—addressed me as "my lady," dropping into a low bow as I neared the stairs. Her hair was much lighter than most of the people I had seen here, and when the light hit it there was a bluish tint to it. I mumbled a hasty good morning around my mouthful of bacon and fled down the three flights of stairs.

I wiped my mouth and hands on the napkin at the bottom of the steps and stuck it in my jeans' pocket. Then looked around realizing I had no clue where the throne room was. I wandered down hallways and into various rooms for a while, surprisingly never running into any other servants. There had been two sitting rooms, a billiards room, a conference room, and a sauna so far. I started to turn down another hall, but the squeaking of a door opening pulled me in the other direction. Maybe there was someone who could help me find the throne room.

This hall was lined with paintings of men and women, the gold plaque at the bottom of each one identifying them as a Kyrion of the past. "Hello," I called out, my voice echoing down the empty hallway. Another creaking noise issued from the open doorway to my right, and I stepped into a library. "Is anyone in here? I could use some directions."

The smell of copper and almonds filled my nose bringing back memories of my father's study. An open walkway divided the room with clusters of tables and comfy-looking chairs dotting each side. A podium and a couple of rows of desks sat near the back wall of windows. Rows of books from thick ancient-looking texts to current novels lined the other three walls. I walked over to one of the tables and picked up a paperback copy of *Oath Taker* by Audrey Grey. Someone had my taste in books. If I ever got a free moment I would come back here and see what other treasures this library held.

I turned toward the door ready to move on when an object in the corner caught my eye. A mechanical clock-like device the size of a beachball sat inside a large glass case. Individual plates of Greek words formed a circle at the center, spinning beneath the feet of five glass figurines of men and women. One of the figurines had been thrust out from the clock face on an extended metal arm. This male figurine was different, filled with an inky black liquid instead of the mercurial gray like the others. Positioned beneath him was one of the words also extended out from the clock face. Luckily, I'd found that one of the perks of my new-found powers was that I could now read multiple languages.

"Faith," I read aloud.

A sound almost like the beating of a heart issued from the clock. Then mechanical gears made whirling and ticking noises as one of the female figurines moved forward a bit. The clock seemed to shudder for a moment as if the gears slipped. I held my breath hoping that this beautiful work of art hadn't broken.

"What are you doing in here?" asked a stern male voice from behind me.

"Holy shitballs," I screeched, jumping out of my skin at the unexpected voice.

I whirled around with my hand holding my galloping heart. A man stood there wearing the black gear like the Talosi but with the House of Chaos symbol covering his torso rather than along his sleeves. He was much older than the soldiers I had met last night. His close-cropped brown hair and short beard were streaked with gray and his dark brown eyes gleamed with murderous rage. The long black sword he held in his left hand was pointed at my chest. "What have you done to the Moirai?" he demanded, pointing to the device with his other hand.

My mouth went dry. "I ... nothing. Talos ... whichever one you are, I swear it just had a little glitch, but it looks like it's working now. See?" I waved toward the glass case where the clock had started up again.

"I am Guide Christos Athan," he said, with a sneer as if I had insulted him by calling him Talos. He glanced at the device before turning his steely eyes back to me. "You can't be in here without permission."

"Sorry," I said, staring down the length of that sword.

"I'm new here. I was looking for the throne room. Selene asked me to meet her there." My hand shook as I reached for my collar and his sword followed the movement. "Maybe you could put the pointy sword down? Look," I pulled the chain from underneath my shirt and let the ring Bennett had given me dangle in the air. "I'm Lia—Kyrion Bennett's bond-mate."

He sheathed his sword but didn't offer an apology. "No one is permitted in here without permission from the Kyrion or Archai."

"Oh, right. Got it." He none too politely ushered me out the door and snapped it closed behind me before locking it with a key he pulled from a chest pocket. I bit the inside of my cheek to keep from lashing out with my building frustration. Everything I'd done since arriving here was wrong. Was this what it was going to be like living here? Walking on eggshells so not to offend anyone and having to ask permission to go places? I swallowed it all down and tried again. "Uh, since you're here do you think you could point me toward the throne room?"

For a moment, I thought he would refuse, then he gave me an awkward bow that seemed forced. "This way, my lady."

6

I followed the guide down the long hallway until the wooden floors gave way to rough stone and a wide set of open wooden doors appeared. We stepped into a large rectangular room of stone. Directly across from where I stood a set of steps led up to a platform with two black thrones. Tall wooden double doors stood on either side of the platform. Banners with symbols from all six Houses hung from wooden rafters far above. The sun shone through stained-glass windows which lined the second and third floor balconies overlooking the space, and a variety of colors spilled across the stone floor. This must be the old section of the house that I'd noticed last night.

Selene was sitting at a wooden desk placed in the center of the room, signing documents and sorting them into neat stacks.

"I apologize for interrupting you, Archai," Guide Athan proclaimed with reverence and a deep bow. "My lady, Jillian Davies, has finally arrived."

Sure, suck up to the boss lady, I mentally grumbled. And

did they have to keep calling me Jillian? It was so stuffy sounding, but that's probably why they liked it.

"Thank you, Christos." Selene acknowledged him without looking up. "Will you inform Modístra Althaia that Ms. Davies' measurements will have to be taken from her other clothes as we will not be able to keep our appointment with her today?"

"It will be done at once, Archai." Christos Athan snapped another curt bow, all traces of the belligerence he had shown me gone in his eagerness to please Selene. Then he left with a pep in his step that hadn't been there before.

Someone is a kiss-ass, I mentally smirked, until I remembered that I'd wasted two hours of Selene's time by showing up late. Guess it was my turn to pucker up.

"I'm sorry I'm late. I overslept, and then I couldn't find the room," I blurted while Selene continued to ignore me as she signed several pages of what looked like invoices. "I accidentally stumbled into the library. Then I saw the clock and lost track of time." I pressed my hands nervously to my thighs as Selene's head snapped up and the pen she had been writing with fell from her hand.

"What did you say?"

"I'm sorry I'm late," I ventured again as she put her hands on the desk and stood up staring at me with such intensity my skin tingled. Her hair was pulled back into a high ponytail and she wore all black similar to the gear that the soldiers wore minus the weapons. Her House of Chaos mark sat prominently between her breasts displayed by the V-cut of the armor she wore. Molly—the girl who had been my guide during the Games and had once been my friend—had explained to me that the positioning of the symbol on the torso was a measure of a Paldimori's power: the higher the position, the more powerful they were. Selene was apparently near the top of the power-chain.

"No, the other part, about the library," Selene prompted. "How did you get in?"

"Uh, I walked in. The doors were open. Sorry, I didn't know I needed to get permission."

The silence stretched on for an uncomfortable minute until I realized she was speaking telepathically with someone. "That room was locked as it normally is. The Talos on duty says he checked it himself only minutes before Guide Athan found you there."

I remembered how the elevator at Titan Tower had taken me to the library during the first competition of the Games. Later Bennett had told me that there wasn't a number in the elevator that corresponded with that floor. "Libraries in your world seem to like me." I shrugged.

"Guide Athan says that you did something to the Moirai." Selene's lips pinched tight. "Is that true, Lia?"

I noticed that she didn't call me "my lady" like everyone else but maybe she was high enough rank that she didn't have to. "No!" I replied in irritation at the guide for tattling on me when it wasn't even my fault. "I told him I didn't do anything to the clock. It just hiccupped for a minute but it's fine."

"The Moirai doesn't 'hiccup.' That clock was made by the first Kyrion Erebus himself when the Games were founded. It counts down the months remaining to complete all six competitions." Selene explained with barely concealed ire. That must have been why there were only four metal pieces with numbers still turning on the clock; there were only four months left in the year. "Never before have the figurines moved or changed color. And never has that clock had a 'hiccup' in all the thousands of years since it was created. Yet both of those things have occurred since you bonded with Bennett."

Great! I was like a bad omen that equaled apocalyptic-level on the oh-shit meter to these people. "I don't know why that happened. I didn't mean to break your clock." Guilt and worry ate at me causing my powers to flare and sparks flew from my fingertips. "I didn't mean to insult your servants or break your laws." Those angry fireflies took flight again, stinging my veins and scorching my chest. "I don't know why I'm the first Chosen ever, or what any of this means. I didn't mean to hurt Dia or Molly." Sweat beaded my brow as my chest heaved and every wrong move I'd made that led me here crashed over me. "Now James is dead and Grace too. I can't find the twin Houses no matter how much I research, and time is running out. I never wanted any of this!"

Fireballs shot from each of my hands spinning crazily out into the room. I watched in horror as Selene calmly straightened and jumped over the desk kicking it back away from her. The table slid about twenty feet away as Selene held out her hand and caught the first ball of fire as if we were playing catch. She spun and leaped into the air, impossibly high. The ball of fire in her hand turned into a whip that she lashed at one of the other balls that was speeding toward the banners hanging from the ceiling. The crack of the fire whip disintegrated the speeding ball leaving behind tiny embers that floated harmlessly to the ground. Selene landed in a crouch and spun quickly in the direction of the other ball that was speeding toward the thrones, sketching a symbol in the air. A shield of rippling waves of heat formed like a wall in front of the platform, and the last ball of fire started to lose its form as it stretched and elongated before being absorbed into the shield.

I dropped to my knees as the heat inside me dissipated, leaving me feeling cold and empty. "I-I'm sorry," I said quietly as Selene approached with that fire whip still clutched in her hands. I didn't move as I waited for the lashes to strike. I deserved it. I had broken my word to her about being here at dawn and lost control of my powers proving that I was too incompetent to ever be a Kyrion.

Selene stopped before me, extinguishing her whip. "A Kyrion only kneels to our gods." She offered me a hand and pulled me to my feet. "A Kyrion is always in control of themselves and their surroundings." She looked at something over my shoulder, her lips pressed into a thin line of discontent. Her hand snapped out, and I stumbled backward thinking she was going to hit me. Something flew by my head, and she snagged it out of the air. I turned toward the entrance behind me, surprised to find Bennett there. For a brief moment I could swear I saw sadness and regret lining his face but then it was gone, and I was staring at the cold mask of Kyrion Chaos.

"Remember that I love you, Lia," Bennett said through our connection, *"no matter what I must do to keep you safe."* He nodded to Selene and then left without another word. An uneasy feeling settled in my stomach. He had to have seen my loss of control. He was a born protector, taking on the responsibility of trying to keep everyone around him safe. But how far would he go to achieve that? There was definitely something I was missing.

"Here," Selene said pulling my troubled gaze back to her, "you will wear this during our lessons until you learn to control your powers."

She handed me a silver cuff of leaves. I slipped it around my wrist and pushed it up my arm until it fit snuggly around my bicep. The moment it settled into place it felt as though my powers were being suffocated beneath a heavy blanket. The absence of my powers felt as if I had lost a limb but could still feel the phantom sensation of where it should be. It was extremely uncomfortable. I hadn't realized until this moment how accustomed I'd become to the presence of my powers until they were locked away. I wanted to rip the cuff off my arm and hurl it as far away from me as possible.

"What is this thing?"

Selene glanced briefly at the cuff. From her pinched expression, it appeared that she wasn't a fan of the pretty piece of jewelry either. "It's called a *kóvo*," she replied. "It basically puts your powers to sleep so that you can't trigger them." She must have noticed my puzzled look. "We use them to subdue criminals. Once it's locked into place, it can only be removed by a Kyrion, Kafàli, or Archai.

"Time, as you said, is running out, let us continue your lessons." Selene motioned for me to follow her and we skirted around the mess of papers scattered across the floor. I wanted to stop to pick them up, but I didn't want to cause another scene so I followed obediently behind her. She stopped at the base of the steps in front of the thrones and turned to me. "Do you know why our Kyrion are important, Lia?"

"Because people need structure and leaders to guide them." I answered thinking about my years as a business owner.

"That is a very human answer," Selene replied, sounding as if she wasn't surprised. "We need our Kyrion for survival. When the gods roamed this earth, they were our connection to the God of Chaos. It was through them that our powers flowed giving us greater strength. Before the gods disappeared, they imbued six gems with their powers and gifted them to their strongest descendants. Those descendants became the first Kyrion." She motioned to one of the scenes depicted in the stained-glass windows that showed the six gems being passed down. "Our powers sustain our world. When you become Kyrion it is a *promise* to hold and guard that lifeline for all descendants of the House of Chaos. In *thirteen* days, you will make that pledge at the coronation. It is a duty that can only be passed on when the next person is blessed with the Kyrion symbol by the God of Chaos."

It wasn't lost on me that she called me out on promises made, and the fact that I had lost hours of time for training because of my tardiness. She was questioning how she could trust me with the safety of her people when I couldn't even keep a simple promise to meet with her here for our lesson. I didn't have an answer for her. Until she spelled it out so clearly, I hadn't really thought of what my life as a Kyrion would be like. Somehow, I thought I would suffer through the ceremony and then go on as I had been doing, trying to complete my quest and find answers about my family. But now I was wondering how I was going to be able to do that in addition to my duties as Kyrion.

"I'm sorry," I said solemnly, rubbing my sweaty palms on my jeans. Beyond her shoulder the black thrones seemed to taunt me. Selene made this all look so effortless, while I bumbled my way through. I didn't know if I'd ever deserve to sit on one of those thrones, but for Bennett's sake I was going to try. "I'm here now, if you have a little more time to teach me today?"

I tried not to squirm under her cool assessment. Finally, she nodded.

"This throne," Selene motioned to the smaller of the two black thrones on the platform, "has sat empty since Bennett's mother, Calidora, died."

I winced recalling the conversation I'd had with Lydia.

No wonder she had looked at me as if I'd committed a cardinal sin. She had been talking about Bennett's *mother* when she kept mentioning Kyrion Calidora. I'd called the woman a dress lover and said I was nothing like her. I hoped to whatever gods were listening that my gaffe wouldn't end up in the rumor mill and make it back to Bennett or Selene.

Selene continued on oblivious to my mortification, "Kyrion Calidora was loved by all of our people. She was not only powerful but courageous. Daring to change some of our laws and bring us a more contemporary way of life. She wanted her people to be happy and healthy above all else. She left her mark on the history of our House." Selene waved an elegant hand toward another section of stained-glass windows that showed people in fields struggling to raise crops at the mercy of harsh weather. In the next, the people looked healthy as they accepted packages from what appeared to be the runners Lydia had mentioned.

"Kyrion Calidora was the last of the arranged marriages. She wanted more for her son and future Kyrion than a life of duty." A deep love and admiration were evident in Selene's voice as she looked at the smaller throne. "Our mothers were best friends, and Kyrion Calidora treated me like a daughter. She believed in me and fought to give me a chance to fill the role of Archai even though it had never been held by a woman before."

Selene turned to me, those sharp golden eyes seeming to pierce through to my soul. My head pounded as I felt a pressure pushing against my brain, and I swayed on my feet. Then it was gone. I blinked, confused, but Selene only nodded. "Good, you have strong shields," she stated like she had finally found one redeeming quality in me. "Kyrion Calidora is the type of leader our people deserve. She raised Bear to be like her, and he is worth ten of any of the other

Kyrion alive today." As composed as Selene looked, it was her eyes that gave her away. A storm raged there, promising pain and retribution to anyone who threatened those she loved. "We are all fiercely loyal to him."

Message received loud and clear. "I do want to be what our people deserve, and I would *never* hurt Bennett."

"That's a promise that I'll hold you to," she said coldly.

7

"To be a Kyrion, you must look and act like one," Selene instructed as she paced around me with her hands behind her back. "A servant will bring one of the dresses the runners bought for you to change into. For now, let's start with the pledge that you will make at the coronation."

"What about the bonding thing, isn't that coming up, like, tomorrow?"

"The Bonding Ceremony is very straightforward, but I'll write down what you will need to say. It's only a formality, really, to declare your intentions toward each other. You'll say the words I give you with Bear as you ascend each step of the bonding altar. Just remember that you control the fire, it doesn't control you." Selene dismissed the bonding as if it were no big deal, but it sounded like we were getting engaged in front of the entire city. That was not a small thing in my book. If I'd learned anything since coming here, it was that I was woefully unprepared for becoming a full-fledged member of the Paldimori society and the chances of me screwing up that ceremony were high.

"It's the coronation that you need to worry about,"

Selene said, "since that will be when you will have to prove yourself fit to be Kyrion. It is also your responsibility to plan it, and you need to make arrangements immediately."

My mouth fell open as I stared at her incredulously. Gallery exhibitions I could plan, but big fancy ceremonies —? Uh-uh, no way.

"Now, repeat after me," Selene commanded, ignoring my impending panic attack. "I am a child of the God of Chaos. I was brought to this earth to bring balance. I am the light. I am the dark. To neither extreme shall I devote myself fully. I am all things as my duty demands. I vow to lead my people with courage and honor until the God of Chaos claims my successor. To the God of Chaos, I pledge myself, Kyrion Jillian Nova Davies of the House of Chaos."

I repeated the pledge several times with Selene correcting me when I got parts of it wrong.

"Now that I can say it, what does it mean?" I had told myself I was going to keep my mouth shut no matter what, but if I was going to sign my life away to do this job, I wanted to know the fine print. "That 'I am the dark' part doesn't sound like a good thing. I'm not going to the dark side for anyone."

Selene paused her pacing, looking irritated at my interruption for a moment before she donned that Diplomatic Doll countenance. "This world was never meant to sustain a utopian society. There are many who think that's why our original home was destroyed, and our people went to war. That our ancestors strayed too far toward the light and the God of Chaos punished us." She motioned to another of the stained-glass windows where a bloody battle was taking place. "We are all—humans and Paldimori alike—imperfect. We all have different motivations and beliefs. One person's idea of utopia can be another's nightmare. Look at all the evil Hitler did, trying to achieve his version of perfection. We stepped in to help stop him, as we have stopped others before him. We intervene where we think we must in the human world, but we don't have to create acts of evil. There's enough of that already happening." Selene sighed, looking tired. It was the first real emotion I'd seen her openly display. Then she was back to being stoic. "The point is that a Kyrion has to make hard decisions for the good of their people."

"Can't they make good decisions without wading into the dark side?"

"Would you do something that felt wrong if you thought it was the best way to keep your friend safe?" Selene turned to greet Lydia, who bustled in with a dress draped over her arms. A second servant brought in a pile of books and set them carefully on the desk. While Selene gave the servants orders, I stewed over her question. Keeping secrets from my best friend hadn't felt right but I had done it thinking I was keeping her safe. Maybe I wasn't as far from the dark side as I thought.

I found myself standing on that lonely highway inside me where I once buried my thoughts and emotions until I had nearly become a vacant shell. The sun peeked over the horizon, its rays reaching for the crumbling highway that stretched out in the distance, but not quite reaching it yet. Green grass dotted the once-barren landscape in small clumps. A resilient wildflower struggled to grow here and there. A viscous liquid dripped from my right hand onto the only remaining section of well-maintained pavement beneath my feet. I knew what I would find when I looked down, but no matter how hard I tried I could never stop myself from looking. My eyes drifted slowly down to the bloody knife in my hand. The pavement beneath me trembled as if a giant beast were trying to break through. The pavement cracked and started to tear. The knife disappeared as I dropped to my knees and pushed at the pavement trying to stop the crack from spreading. My hands cut and bled, mixing with the blood of the man whose lifeless eyes I could never forget. Finally, the trembling stopped as the crack sealed over with blood.

"You do not belong here." Whispered across the land in that same voice I had heard in my room this morning. *"Go now."*

A hand clamped onto my arm pulling me back to the present. I hadn't realized I'd bent over to help the servant picking up the papers scattered across the floor. Selene pulled me away and steered me toward the tall wooden doors to the right of the thrones. "You must forget your human instincts," she admonished quietly. "Each person in a House has a role to fulfill. Roles in direct service to the Kyrion are highly sought after and are a great honor when awarded. You are saying that a servant is unfit for their role if you help them." Selene pushed the door open and motioned Lydia to follow us. We stepped through the doors into a short hallway with two more doors at the end. Selene asked Lydia to go prepare my dress, then turned to me after the servant disappeared behind the door on the left. "Be careful, Lia. Laws still exist to punish anyone barring a person from performing their duties." Selene's grip on my arm had tightened to a painful level. When I shifted uneasily, she released me quickly and stepped back as if she hadn't even realized she was still holding onto me. "Follow Lydia, and she will help you change into your dress."

What felt like hours later I stepped back through the doorway into the throne room. Being dressed by someone else wasn't an experience I wanted to repeat. The scattered papers had been removed from the floor of the throne room, but the desk still stood in the middle with the books stacked on top. Voices drifted toward me, and I found Selene standing with Talos Gavril at the base of the steps leading up to the thrones.

"There was an attack just beyond the eastern tower," the soldier reported.

"Did we lose anyone?" Selene asked, standing ramrod straight with her hands clasped behind her.

"Two runners who must have been caught by surprise," Talos Gavril answered with a grim look.

"Are the towers secure?"

"For now, Archai," Talos Gavril's voice dropped until I could barely hear it. "They are getting closer and bolder."

I stepped forward hoping to hear more and the damn robe swished across the floor catching their attention. Talos Gavril bowed to me, and Selene instructed me how to acknowledge him by making a hand motion in the air almost like drawing a triangle with a swooping ending. Now I knew why the servant on the stairs had nearly fallen when she bowed, and I only nodded to her with my mouth full of bacon and walked away. Apparently, a bow made directly in front of a Kyrion was a form of displaying loyalty and commitment, whereas a bow made off to the side or while backing away was simply respectful. I wanted to pull my hair out with all of these rules!

Talos Gavril left after another lesson on dismissing someone from my presence. Selene walked out with him speaking too softly this time for me to overhear what they were discussing. I waited by the desk and peeked around the room to make sure I was alone before taking off the robe and setting it on the desk. My long-sleeved black dress had red pleats that you couldn't really see until I was walking—

or spinning. I turned in a quick spin and the bell skirt flared out around me, flashing red and black. The material was surprisingly soft and lightweight. Thankfully, with the weight I'd lost over the last several months, my thighs weren't in danger of starting a friction fire. I could almost like it. But it was the black hooded robe that the Kyrion wore to official ceremonies that was giving me trouble. I stopped spinning and grimaced down at the robe. The long hem had trailed along the ground making me trip several times in the hallway when I was coming back to the throne room.

"Now you almost look the part," Selene said as she joined me. I slipped the robe back on and she nodded in approval. "Lydia will have something more formal brought to your room this evening for our meeting with the ladies you will need to work with for the coronation plans. We'll meet in the dining hall for dinner at 6 p.m. and then move to the sitting room across the hall. Don't be late. Now let's see if we can teach you what you'll need to know."

Selene raised her hand and the stack of books floated up from the desk. Each of the ten books opened to a certain page as they took up position floating in a circle around me. On the page of the book in front of me was an ancestry tree for the Kyrion line of the House of Chaos. My finger traced down the branches of Bennett's family, stopping on his mother's name. Next to her name was a picture of the woman in the painting over my bed. Of course! Now that I had made the connection, I wondered how I'd missed the resemblance before. Mother and son shared the same eye shape, straight-edged nose, and high cheekbones.

Doubt overwhelmed me. How the hell was I ever going to measure up to either one of them? From all I'd heard, they were basically saints. In my mind's eye, I found myself back on the crumbling pavement of my lonely highway.

Only now there was a fork in the road ahead that I didn't remember being there before. In one direction, the highway ended abruptly in a wall of swirling mists. In the other direction, the road disappeared into a forest where the first rays of the sunrise were struggling to peek through the dense leaves. Neither option looked appealing, but when I turned back around, the pavement behind me had vanished.

Unsettled, I stepped back and stumbled again on the black robe nearly falling. Selene sighed and waved her hand to shoo the books out of the way. "Take the robe off and hold it out to your side."

I did as she asked, expecting this was some fresh new hell I was going to be put through. The biggest sword I had ever seen appeared in Selene's hands as she walked toward me with a look of determination. I gulped heavily as she raised the sword and swung it so close to me that I could feel the wind ruffle my skirt. A section of the robe fluttered to the floor. My knees knocked together in terror as the sword disappeared once more into thin air. "Now you should be able to walk without tripping," she said.

Holy gods, she's like She-Ra in black battle gear.

"Uhm, thanks," I gulped.

Selene nodded, then waved the books back into place. I scratched at the metal cuff around my bicep wondering if I would ever manage to control my powers the way she did with such ease. Then I had no more time to think as she tried to cram as much knowledge into my brain as possible in the short time we had. Luckily, I was much better at visual learning and picked up on the House hierarchies and territories from the books fairly quickly. There was even a slight nod of approval from Selene on that part of my lessons.

Two hours later, I stumbled into my bedroom. Grayson must have arrived because Click was in the middle of the floor surrounded by scattered pieces of his favorite stationery with the silhouette of a dancing couple across the top. The young servant with the blue-tinted hair sat on the floor giggling as Click showed off his dance moves. She quickly scrambled to her feet when she noticed me and backed out the door, bowing the whole way. The pen flew over to me clicking happily as he showed me his drawing of the feather duster he was currently crushing on. I mumbled praises and told him to clean up his mess before falling face down on the bed. My brain felt numb from all of the laws, family names, roles, and proper etiquette floating around inside. My legs and back hurt from standing over those books for so long. And tomorrow we would be doing this all over again.

I groaned and pulled the pillow over my head.

8

"Lia, wake up." Bennett shook my shoulder, and I burrowed deeper into my pillow. I think I grumbled something like "get fucked" but was too tired to care. My dreams had been plagued by the Moirai ticking away in the background as Titan urged me to find the twin Houses, and the mysterious voice I kept hearing telling me I needed to leave. Bennett chuckled and kissed the back of my neck. "Come on, aster-àki, it is time to train those unruly powers."

"No," I huffed. "Go away. My head hurts, and it's all your adviser's fault. That makes it your fault too."

Bennett massaged my aching back. "Does this make up for turning Selene loose on you?"

I made happy groaning noises. Bennett continued the massage a few more minutes, then rolled me onto my back. He leaned down to place a quick kiss on my lips, then pulled me to my feet.

I grumbled all the way down to the basement training room. At the far end of the room was a swimming pool and hot tub. On the other side of the room all of the exercise equipment had been pushed up against the wall of the gym area, leaving the floor in front of the mirrors bare except for a couple of mats.

"Isn't Grayson training with us today?" I asked, rubbing my arm where the kóvo had been. Selene had taken it back after our lesson, but it left an icky feeling behind.

"No, Grayson is working on something else at the moment. This time it will only be you and me," Bennett responded. Something sounded off about his voice, but I let it go. "We will start with sparring."

"Fine," I said around a yawn.

We stepped onto the mats, and Bennett swept my feet out from under me before I knew what was happening.

"Ouch! I think my kidneys just cried surrender."

"Get up," Bennett commanded. "Again."

"Ok, geez. Are you having a bad day or something? I'm completely fine with rescheduling."

I barely made it too my feet before a fist landed in my stomach. He had pulled the punch, but it still knocked the breath out of me.

"Get your hands up. Block me," Bennett demanded, landing another blow to my thigh. "Will you surrender this easily to our enemies? No wonder Natalie found you such an easy target. You let her destroy your reputation and your business."

"Bennett, what ..." A vision invaded my head, ripping me from my stunned stupor in Bennett's gym to my old office at my art gallery in Port Lawson. I watched as the woman I had been nearly four months ago sobbed at her desk. The anguished sounds of her despair filled the room, and, suddenly, I was her again. All of those feelings poured into me—helplessness, anger, and grief. Then I was back in the gym. A fireball surrounded my hand and was aimed at Bennett's chest.

"Get out of here!" I shouted, so afraid that I would hurt him. My fear fed the power and the ball got bigger. "Run before I lose control!"

"Focus on the power at your center. Hold it tight in your grasp and reverse the flow," Bennett instructed, completely ignoring my pleas that he leave. "You cannot run from this. The power is a part of you. Embrace it and control it."

I closed my eyes and searched out the power at my center. A giant ball of light as bright as the sun spun, throwing off flares of dark red. Other colors writhed and pushed against the surface as if looking for a way out. It was chaos. How could you control something that had no rhyme or reason?

I pictured myself wrapping my hands around the ball, trying to shove the escaping flares back inside. As soon as I shoved one in, another appeared. What had Bennett said? Hold it tight and reverse the flow. I hugged the glowing ball to me, and the world exploded. My back hit the mat with a thud, and my eyes flew open to see scorched ceiling tiles above me.

"Bennett!" I rolled over frantically searching for him, afraid of what I might find. He stood on a perfectly preserved circle of the mat, not a hair out of place. The rest of the mat was a melted mess around us.

"The fire is mine to command, Lia. Never forget that." His cold gaze swept over me sending a chill down my spine. I remembered that gaze very well. This wasn't my Bennett standing in front of me now, but Kyrion Chaos. "You will get on your feet, Potential, and do it again until you can no longer stand."

9

I had never been afraid of Bennett but there was a harsh desperation to our training today that made me think of his words earlier in the throne room. *"Remember that I love you, Lia, no matter what I must do to keep you safe."*

I had wondered how far he would go to protect me and now I think I had my answer.

"Bennett—"

Five servants entered the room carrying in new mats. "Replace the mats and leave," he ordered.

I moved well out of the way and crossed my arms as I leaned against the wall. The tension in the air was thick enough to cut with a knife, and the servants kept looking at me suspiciously. *"Bennett, don't take your anger with me out on them,"* I requested through our connection.

The servants wrapped up quickly as ordered and bowed deeply to Bennett. They bowed respectfully to me, but I could see they blamed me for the abrupt behavior of their beloved leader. *"Can you please tell them we're training? They're looking at me like I attacked you and they want to cut off my head."*

"Wait," he called out to the servants as they neared the door. They all stopped immediately, patiently awaiting their orders. "Thank you for bringing fresh mats. We will take a break from our training in one hour. Please bring water and a light snack."

"It will be done, Kyrion Bennett," they chorused with bows and left somewhat mollified.

The silence stretched out between us as we watched each other warily. I hated that there was a distance between us now that hadn't been there before we came here. "Is this one of the things you think—"

"We need to get back to training," Bennett commanded.

I sighed and pushed off the wall to join him on the mats once more. We were definitely going to talk later.

"Do you remember him?" Bennett held up his hand and a picture appeared. It was of a teenager with his arms wrapped around two little boys all with the same dark hair and crooked smiles.

The shift in our training and the picture of the boy who haunted my dreams caught me off guard. "James," I replied in a raspy whisper, attempting to swallow down the tightness in my throat as sorrow threatened to choke me. Natalie had used the teenager who had been caring for my parents' house to get to me. It was her anger at me that had made her blast the chair James was tied to through the portal in my father's library, breaking his neck. A deep rumbling sound issued from under the pavement of my lonely highway. The asphalt split, spewing dirt and smoke into the air. Guilt and regret poured into me, tearing the words that I had been suppressing for weeks from my lips. I choked out, "That's the boy that I k-killed."

Bennett's fingers tightened around the photo. His lips pressed into a hard line as if he wanted to say something but was holding himself back. He had told me many times that James's death wasn't my fault but that didn't stop me from feeling responsible. *If only I had been smarter. If only my stupid powers had come with an instruction manual that I could follow, I could have protected us all that day.*

My powers flared, threatening to incinerate everything around me. I envisioned a shield as if there was an impenetrable bubble of glass surrounding that burning ball of light inside me. I painstakingly molded it as if it were one of my glass sculptures, shaping it around my powers and holding it there with sheer determination. Flares of red pushed against the transparent shield, but it held. I exhaled a shaky breath of relief. It was working!

The air shifted. That was the only warning I got before Bennett teleported directly in front of me. His fist shot toward me, and I ducked just in time. His knee drove up toward my face; I dodged to the left and dropped to the ground. My foot swept out toward the back of his knee, but he had already teleported across the gym. I quickly got back on my feet, the deadly look on Bennett's face sending chills down my spine as he launched a ball of fire at me.

I teleported and nearly fell over a weight bench as I stumbled backward, still struggling with sticking my landings. Bennett was nowhere to be seen, but the heat along the symbol on my back let me know he was still near.

Where the hell is he?

Bennett's voice whispered next to my ear, "Do you think Natalie would have taken it this easy on you?"

I spun around but no one was there. "What is this?"

"This is the shadows. They are an extension of Thanatos —the shadowlands of the dead. The in-between place where souls sometimes linger before they are sent to one of the other levels of the underworld." Bennett's voice sounded behind me, and I shifted in that direction. "When you learn how to use them, you can become invisible to your enemies. But you, Potential Davies, never learn, do you?"

Suddenly, I was flying backwards. My back hit the mat hard, knocking the breath from me. Bennett appeared again, leaning over my prone form. "You let your guard down again. Do you think our enemies will let you call time-out to get those unruly powers under control?" He pressed his hand against my throat and used his powers to pull me up into the air until I was dangling in his grip. He was being careful not to do any real damage, but I couldn't move. His eyes blazed up at me as he sneered, "They will cut you down in an instant without a care that you are the almighty Chosen." The arrogant mask of the Kyrion stared up at me mockingly. "Will you hang here all day, or do you plan to *do* something?"

Anger lit up a flare so quickly inside me that fire ignited around my hands. I reached for my shield and found a section had melted. Those angry red flares were escaping, wanting to burn everything around me. Dammit, Bennett had distracted me, and I had lost my concentration on the shield.

"Temper, temper," Bennett taunted me.

I reached for the glass-like surface to fix the hole when the air stirred, and I was flying across the room. My stomach dropped as I was flipped around in the air in some kind of demented ballet. I sucked in a deep breath, trying my best to repair the shield around my powers while being tossed around the room.

"Trapping your power will not protect you, Potential." Bennett's angry voice echoed off the walls of the gym. "Do something with it!"

My feet finally touched the ground, and I fell to my

knees, too dizzy to stand. Between one breath and the next, I was somewhere else. An anguished bellow rang through the air of the flower field where I had competed in the first competition of the Games. Groups of people huddled together watching a kneeling man holding a woman in his arms. The man kissed the woman gently and laid her down on the ground. I walked closer, and my knees almost gave out. Bennett stood and turned to the crowd, but I couldn't take my eyes off the body on the ground. My own sightless eyes stared up from a blood and dirt-streaked face, and blood flowed from the hole where the arrow had struck me.

Bennett bellowed at the crowd behind me, and I dragged my attention away from my dead body to see what was happening. Bennett's face was consumed with a manic rage I had never seen before. He glanced over at my dead body, his eyes full of mindless devastation. This must have been what happened after I died. But how did I get here?

The cracks in my lonely highway opened wider and another wave of grief hit me. My powers surged up and burst out of me.

In the next breath I found myself back in the gym, lying face down on the mats feeling wrung out from the emotional rollercoaster ride. The perfect imprint of my hands was burned into the mat beneath me. Fire lit up my hands and climbed up my arms. I pushed to my feet quickly trying to keep my powers from slipping any further beyond my control.

Bennett stood in a wide-legged stance several feet away watching me. Then he launched himself at me like a freight train, and I barely avoided the foot he aimed at my ribs. He pursued me across the mats never letting up. For every punch or kick I blocked, twice as many made contact. Even without the full force of his blows, my body was aching all over. My fire raged hotter, flaring out around me to singe the walls. He left me no time to gain my focus or rebuild my shield. All I could do was react as he continued to attack.

"Are you even trying, Potential?" Bennett asked in that condescending tone he had used when we first met.

My elbow connected with air as he teleported away. An arm banded around my middle, and he teleported us to the back of the gym, his muscular body pressed menacingly all along mine. My cheek smashed up against the mirrors; my hands trapped between my body and the glass. One calloused hand gripped my neck, the other my thigh. Another picture slammed itself against the mirror inches from my nose and hung there taunting me. The auburn-haired woman in the photo was laughing as a skinny kid with choppy hair and a stubborn look of determination tried to lift a huge sword.

"You remember Grace, right?" Bennett's lips brushed along my ear. "The woman that died during the first competition? I know you remember the adopted daughter she left behind. Molly was such a stubborn little thing even then."

My heart clenched, and my panting breaths hitched. I was back in the flower field as another image filled my head of Molly West kneeling over my dead body, sobbing. A scream pierced the air, and Grace's body fell to the ground, her neck bent at an odd angle. Molly stumbled away from my body to throw herself across Grace's lifeless form, sobbing even harder.

Then I was back in the gym once more with my ragged breaths fogging the mirror as I struggled to bank the fire that was now licking up its surface. Another photo slammed against the glass. This was a more recent picture of Molly—the girl who had become my friend before I had gotten her mother killed.

"Is this the friend you *abandoned* to mourn you and her mother?" Bennett asked coldly, watching me squirm as if I were a bug on a windshield. "Your healing powers brought you back from the brink of death. But you never told Molly that, did you? She did not take the news of your return to the island well."

No, she hadn't. Grief and regret filled me until my skin felt too uncomfortable to contain me. I had never gotten to tell Molly I was still alive, or how sorry I was for her mother's death. There had been a brief moment of shock and happiness on Molly's face when I had returned to Sotiria days ago. That had quickly been replaced by a seething hatred, and then an icy wall of indifference as she walked away without a word. I couldn't blame her. Bennett had kicked me off the island for my own safety after I had recovered from the arrow wound, but Natalie had found me and tried to kill me again. Then I had been in training trying to control my powers, so I didn't accidentally kill someone. All that time had passed, and I had never reached out to Molly. Now it was too late, and there was no excuse in the world that was going to make things ok between us. But I wasn't going to stop trying to reach Molly—or Dia.

Power burned through my veins as the anger, fear, and pain ripped up portions of my lonely highway, leaving me exposed. In my mind, white light poured from my eyes again as I floated off the ground. Bennett stood beside me with his arms folded across his chest. "All of our lives are in your hands. Save us, Chosen."

The power swelled in me, feeding off the tidal wave of emotions. My shield lay in broken shards: the glass not strong enough to contain it any longer. Flares of white and red power lashed at me, looking for a way out. All the emotions pouring through me teased around the lights, stoking them higher. There was no way to close this Pandora's box. *If only I could teleport away somewhere that I couldn't hurt anyone.*

But that wouldn't solve the problem because the problem was me. It was time I hung up my running shoes. The power was inside me. It wasn't like I could just rip it out. *Holy shit! That's it.* I had been trying all this time to box it in, just like I had stuffed my emotions under my highway. Neither were meant to be imprisoned. The words Bennett had said to me earlier echoed through my head: *"The power is a part of you. Embrace it and control it."*

Instead of trying to put a shield around my emotions and my powers, I braided them together. Strands of anger, grief, and pain, I wove with the red flares of power. I stared in awe as my powers stopped fighting me. Before I could rethink my actions, I pulled open the door on my side of our connection. Bennett materialized at the threshold of his door, watching me closely. I held my chaotic ball of emotion-fueled powers in my hands. My gaze never broke from his as I held out my hands, offering him the powers he had wanted months ago when he tricked me into forming this bond. Now through our bond, I felt his surprise and his reluctance.

"I do not want your powers, Lia," he said.

"*I know you would never take them from me now*," I responded. I had been cautiously dipping my toe into this relationship waiting to get hurt again, but I couldn't keep doing that to us. I needed to find a way past my own insecurities and fears. My love for this man was no small thing: it felt as vast and endless as the heavens. We were connected on every level, and it was time I stopped denying that. *"I'm asking you to help me. To share the powers and show me how to use them."*

A smile lit up Bennett's face, and he reached for me. His calloused hands wrapped around mine, and the light pulsed between us as if it too was happy. Bennett didn't try to force the light in any direction, mold it, or suppress it as I had done. He simply let it sink into him, caressing it, almost as if he were petting an animal. When he had gotten a feel for the power, his movements turned fluid and sure as he slowly began to pull on it. The power shot out through his body, filling him and shifting wherever he commanded. I copied his movements, and the power flowed through me, lighting up every cell of my body. I held up my hand and a flame flickered on my palm. Bennett smiled at me with pride. I had missed his smile so much.

I pulled on more of the power, but it came forward too quickly. Suddenly, I was back in the Emerald Rainforest watching Dia being claimed by the Goddess Gaia. Her blood rained down on the ground; her mouth stretched wide in a silent scream. The power swelled through my body and burst out of me in a wave of white-hot fire incinerating everything around me: people, trees, and animals turned to ash before my eyes. Then I was back in the gym, my screams bouncing off the concrete walls. Bennett's strong arms were around me rocking me back and forth.

"It is not real, Lia. It is not real. Dia is fine. They are all fine. You did not hurt anyone."

"I killed ..." My hoarse voice tapered off into nothing.

"It was a dreamscape," Bennett explained, cupping my face in his hands and forcing me to focus on him. "It was not real. I had to reach your true emotions, not the surface that you let me skim."

"I ..." My fingers dug into his forearms to anchor me in the present, as my mind struggled to sort out truth from fiction. "Damn you, Bennett. Don't ever do that to me again!"

We were going to have to talk about our communication issues soon. I knew why he had done what he did, but I was so not ok with it. The dizzying mix of emotions and power I had expended had taken a huge toll. I dropped my head down to my chest, breathing deeply and tried to get my racing heart to calm down. God, that had been awful.

As soon as we finished our training, Bennett was back to being his normal self, but I was finding it hard to switch gears that quickly. How could he go from being the brutal Kyrion to my loving boyfriend so easily? I felt terrible as pain flashed across his face when I flinched away from his kiss, but I couldn't help it.

"I cannot make promises where you are concerned," Bennett declared.

Forcing my emotions to the surface by dredging up all of those bad memories was a calculated move. Selene's words came back to haunt me: "A Kyrion has to make hard decisions for the good of their people." This had all the earmarks of Kyrion Chaos's maneuvering. The problem was I was starting to wonder how much of Bennett was the asshat Kyrion Chaos, and how much of him was the man I had fallen in love with?

"You can't be a dictator about everything. And I'm really emphasizing the 'dick' part here." I scowled at him, releasing my grip on his arms as the tension faded away. "I'll admit that we made progress, but we're gonna have a chat about your methods."

For a moment there my power had become a part of me, and we had worked in unison. That was a huge step forward, not only with my powers, but with our bond. For the first time Bennett and I had worked as a team. It gave me hope that we would work through all other challenges together.

"There are some things I will not negotiate on," Bennett stated firmly. "Your safety is one of them. But I look forward to hearing what will no doubt be your very colorful complaints about my methods," he said wryly and tugged at a sweaty lock of my hair. "The progress you made today was far beyond anything we have achieved in our weeks of training. That was a brilliant move, learning to use your power by watching me through our connection."

"I don't like you very much right now," I grumbled and punched his shoulder. "You better make it up to me with chocolate or orgasms. Actually, I think both will be the price for the torture you put me through."

Bennett pulled me up off the mats as he rose, "I am sure I can work out a repayment schedule."

"Score one for the new kid." I pumped my fist in the air. "I tamed the power beast and earned yummy prizes." We stepped off the mats and I used one of the towels the servants had provided to wipe away the sweat. "Hey, I noticed something when I was reliving when Dia was being claimed. My powers were changing at the same time hers were. That can't be a coincidence."

"No, there are few coincidences where the gods are involved. Do you think the Chosen share a connection similar to the bond?"

"I don't know, but the power that filled me that night was intense. If we get a boost every time a Chosen is claimed, I don't know how I'll ever be able to control it." The grim looks on the faces of the other Kyrion when I had gotten that power boost flashed through my mind. I would be even more dangerous, and the other Kyrion knew it.

10

Bennett had been called away again as soon as we finished training. I refused an escort and took my time coming up the stairs from the basement. A million thoughts rolled through my head about Bennett's behavior, my upcoming 'wedding,' the strange whispers I was hearing, and how I was going to plan a coronation. But overriding them all was an increasing urgency to continue my quest. It nagged at me like a mosquito bite that I was trying desperately not to scratch.

As I neared the middle of the stairs, a cold draft caused me to shiver. Titan's words floated through my head in a lilting female voice. *"Find the twin Houses."* A picture flashed through my mind of two symbols: one a leaping stag silhouetted against a hunter's moon and the second was the sun I had seen in my father's study. The sun symbol for the House of Light—my father's House.

"Go now," whispered that same female voice. The same voice I realized that had been trying to convince me to leave since this morning. The stairwell suddenly went dark and the air heated. A hard shudder wracked my body as it went

from freezing cold to burning hot in only seconds. I struggled to breath in the scorching air as I leaned against the wall for support, dropping to my knees as dry coughs seized my lungs. Then, just as quickly as it had started, it was over.

"My lady," Grayson called, coming into view at the top of the stairs. His boyish smile quickly turned to a look of concern as he spotted me kneeling on the steps and rushed down to help me to my feet. "What has happened, *Adelfi*?" he asked, calling me the Greek word for "sister" in his lightly accented Spanish voice. He had explained that the title meant something more like "one to whom I am sworn to serve and protect above all others."

I hadn't found out until about a week ago when we were sparring, and I had ripped his shirt that Grayson was now marked with a small symbol over his ribs similar to mine where his original House of Shadows symbol once was. The idiot had forsaken his House allegiance and was now bound only to me. I had begged him to undo it, but he had told me he couldn't be released until he had fulfilled his oath. The stubborn ass was going to get himself killed, and I already had too many deaths haunting me. The sight of James's body lying broken in a field of hyacinths filled my mind. Dead eyes, their pale blue staring at me accusingly came next. My eyes prickled with the threat of tears, and I quickly turned away to continue up the stairs. Grayson followed more slowly, checking over the stairwell for any threats.

"I'm ok," I assured him when we reached the top. What had happened on the stairs was suspicious, but I hadn't seen or heard anything to indicate where it came from. I wouldn't make accusations against Bennett's people without some kind of proof. I could only imagine how the people would react to their new Kyrion starting a witch hunt over a hot spot in the basement. "I must have been a little more worn out by training than I thought."

Grayson eyed me for a moment but then nodded. "You have been training hard, my lady. A break would be good." He shifted uncomfortably as if there was something else he wanted to say.

"C'mon, spit it out." I nudged him with my elbow.

"It is not my place to tell you this, my lady, but I think you should know. Kyrion Chaos ..." I held my breath as I waited for Grayson to reveal what Bennett was keeping from me. "He arranged a picnic for you this evening by the hot springs."

"Huh?" That wasn't what I had expected him to say at all.

"He has been trying to abide by your dating agreement, my lady," Grayson's cheeks flushed as he struggled to not give Bennett away.

Relief hit me, and I dropped my arm around Grayson's shoulders giving him a squeeze. Bennett hadn't been hiding some dark secret. He had been taking dating advice and planning our dates with Grayson's help. A giddy feeling of happiness filled me. "Someone has been studying up on dating."

"Uhm, well ..." Grayson seemed flustered for the first time ever.

"It's ok." I laughed and patted his arm. "I knew Bennett was getting pointers from someone. I'd rather it be you than his brother. Jaxon's idea of romance includes cheesy pickup lines and invitations to a hotel room." That was how Jaxon had tried to hit on Dia the first time they'd met. Thoughts of my best friend put a damper on my giddy relief. I couldn't teleport myself back to Sotiria to check on her myself, so I had asked Grayson to do it. He had confirmed she was fine, but I was still worried. *Please keep yourself safe, Dia.*

We moved down the hall toward the grand staircase. "Bennett probably ordered you to provide him a list of things boyfriends are supposed to do. I know the candlelit dinner a couple of weeks ago wasn't his idea. If he becomes an overbearing ass with all the ordering people around that he seems to enjoy, you need to tell me, ok?"

"He is the leader of all Paldimori, my lady." Grayson neatly side-stepped my question. "He was the first ever to be born with the *Archigós*—the supreme leader mark. Kyrion Chaos has been trained since birth in his duties. He is confident and in control at all times, for that is what our people require of him. It is only where you are concerned that he is unsure of himself. If I may make a suggestion, my lady, please be patient with him."

Deep down, I felt a little more of my lonely highway crumble to dust. "He's trying to do things the human way for me; the least I can do is be patient while we both figure this relationship out. Thanks, Grayson," I said, discreetly giving his hand a squeeze in case anyone saw us. I was trying really hard not to break any more of the rules here.

We passed by the hall that led to the library, and I could swear I heard the ticking of that countdown clock. I thought about the symbols I had imagined earlier and made a decision. I couldn't roam around the world looking for the twin Houses right now, but I had somewhere else to finish searching. I pulled away and patted Grayson on the shoulder. "I won't say a word to Bennett that you spilled his little secret but I need you to help me with something."

"My lady, I pledged myself as your personal servant and protector," Grayson said with pride. "As my Kyrion and my Adelfi, I am yours to command."

"How about I just ask nicely?" I smiled mischievously. "Will you please take me to Mercer Island?"

Grayson looked uneasily around the hallway. "I do not think leaving the House grounds is a good idea. I heard the servants talking about attacks along the towers at the base of this mountain. Our enemies have never attacked so openly in broad daylight before."

Grayson motioned for me to walk in front of him as a servant entered the hallway and gave me a passing bow. Several grim-looking Talosi exited the conference room as we were about to pass by. We stopped to watch as they paired off and headed to their assignments. When the doorway cleared, I saw Bennett and Selene facing a wall of monitors. A couple of other people sat at the U-shaped conference table that took up the middle of the room, their attention also on the monitors. The image of a burned-out square tower with bodies lying on the ground filled the TV screens. Men, women, and children—their bodies lying bloody and broken—were stacked up against the wall of the stone tower as if they had tried to huddle there for protection. The body of a Talos guard hung by a noose from the top of the tower, various weapons still embedded in his body, his blood staining the stone wall.

Selene walked over to close the door before I could see anything more. Was this why they were meeting so often? My eyes met Selene's just before the door closed, and I was almost knocked off my feet by the violence lurking there. It was a threat issued loud and clear that whoever had hurt her people would pay.

Grayson and I didn't speak again until we were standing outside my bedroom doors.

"The image on the TV in the conference room," I

ventured hesitantly, "was that from today? What happened?"

"Yes, my lady," Grayson responded looking old beyond his twenty years. "An outcast village in the valley—people who choose not to pledge themselves to this House—were attacked. Several people fled here likely hoping to be granted mercy and taken in, but they only made it as far as one of the guard towers."

My stomach turned at the senseless killing. Our enemies wanted to wipe us from the earth all because the Paldimori were different from them, and they considered us weak. Grayson had once said that the Paldimori were hiding in the shadows. Maybe it was time for them to stop hiding and fight back. It was something to discuss with Bennett later.

"What did you mean when you said they came here looking for mercy?" I waved to indicate this whole big cobbled together mansion that had plenty of room. "They're descendants of the House of Chaos, right? Why wouldn't they stay here?"

Grayson rubbed the back of his neck looking uncomfortable. "The law says that those who refuse to pledge loyalty to a House are considered outcast. They are afforded none of the protections of the House, my lady."

"That's the stupidest thing I've ever heard." My hands landed on my hips as I glared at him. "I'm not pledged to this House either. Are you going to kick me out and leave me for our enemies to torture?"

"Your pledge will be fulfilled when you complete the coronation, my lady." Grayson explained carefully, eyeing my hands where sparks had started to jump into the air. "You are already bonded to the Kyrion, as well as being Chosen. You are unique in our world."

"I won't be treated as an exception when people the

same as me are out there dying." I sucked in a deep breath and held it trying to calm myself down. When I felt I could speak again without lighting the hallway on fire, I continued. "I overheard a conversation between Selene and Talos Gavril. He was saying the enemies are getting closer."

"Yes, my lady," Grayson confirmed. "The attacks are coming more frequently and closer to the home bases."

"Since when? Why wouldn't Bennett tell me about this?" I asked, already guessing what he would say.

Grayson looked away, not wanting to answer.

"Things have started to escalate since the day I was claimed as Chosen, haven't they?" Selene's comments about the clock had been rolling around with all the other issues in my head. Why would the clock have changed when I bonded to Bennett? It didn't make sense. Kyrion had bonded before; there was a whole hall of pictures of the prior leaders. But then I realized Selene wouldn't have known the exact date of our bonding, only that it had happened during the first competition of the Games. I had also been claimed as Chosen during that time, and Bennett was trying to protect me so that I didn't feel like this was my fault. I wasn't taking on that blame though—this was squarely on the shoulders of the gods. "This is all tied together somehow. The Chosen being found, my quest, and the attacks getting worse. I need answers, Grayson. We all do. Help me find them ... please."

He stood taller and looked me in the eye. "I am the first of my family to pledge myself as a *Themis*—an honor-bound protector—in over three centuries. I knew what I was doing when I took my oath, my lady, and I do not regret it. I see in you the salvation of my people even if you do not yet see it for yourself." He bowed deeply to me and chuckled when I hissed at him to cut it out. "I will help you find your answers no matter where they may lie."

"Thank you." I would have hugged him again, but Lydia came around the corner heading our way with an armload of towels. "Oh gods, I'm going to lock myself in the bathroom and shower by *myself*. Teleport to my bedroom in thirty minutes so no one sees you, and we'll leave from there."

"As my lady commands," Grayson said as he backed down the hallway bowing and beaming at me with that boyish grin. I would have thrown my shoe at him if Lydia hadn't been watching disapprovingly. I hurried into the bedroom and shut the door behind me.

11

Click, the spoiled little brat, was sleeping in a velvet-lined jewelry case sitting open on my bed when I entered my bedroom. I had noticed the young servant girl seemed to have developed a friendship with him and assumed she had provided the case. I smiled at the feather he had tucked in beside him from his current crush—a feather duster at my parents' house. Click had been going through a turbulent teenage phase lately. I never knew if I was going to get the horny version trying to "hook up" with various inanimate objects; the rebellious version forging signatures on office supply magazine orders as if they were Playboys; the bratty toddler throwing a tantrum when you cut off his *Dancing with the Stars* marathons; or the sweet kid who liked to draw me cute pictures. I left him to his sleep and rushed into the bathroom.

I showered and dressed, ignoring Lydia's knocking until she finally gave up. When it had been quiet for a few minutes, I peeked out the into the hallway. Grayson waved the all-clear sign from his position near the doors.

I took his hand, and we teleported to my parents'

house. We arrived in the front entrance, and I immediately slumped against the front door trying not to throw up. Having your molecules sucked into a wind tunnel and spat back out again always got to me, especially when someone else was doing the teleporting. Grayson teleported to the kitchen and brought me back a glass of water. I thanked him and sipped slowly as my stomach began to settle. The familiar sights of my childhood home surrounded me, and a heavy weight slipped from my shoulders. Here there were no watchful eyes expecting me to be something I wasn't.

The late day sun streamed in through the wall of windows warming the slate tile of the entrance. The sunken living room to my right with the giant rock fireplace and teal accents brought back memories of nights spent sipping hot chocolate and talking with my mother. To my left was the more formal sitting area with the harp my mother some-times played. Overhead, maple wood beams framed the vaulted ceiling and columns sectioned the areas. A shiver raced down my spine, and I quickly turned away from the wood column that had been replaced after Natalie had smashed me into it. My bones ached momentarily as if remembering the broken bits that my powers had knit back together.

"Are you all right, my lady?" Grayson asked, his too-perceptive gaze soft with sympathy.

I gulped down the last of the water as if it could wash it all away. "I'm fine," I said, forcing a smile as I handed him the empty glass. "I need to look through the rest of the study. I know there's something there, I just have to find it."

"Would you like me to help, my lady?"

"Thanks, Grayson, but I'd like to search by myself for now." He nodded, then escorted me to the study, making sure it was safe before taking off to check the rest of the house and grounds.

The tall sculpture of the anchor from my father's first ship stood near the door. The portal that I'd found right before the confrontation with Natalie took up the left side of the room. The clifftop field of hyacinths that surrounded the tall tower in the distance with its glowing ball of orangish-yellow light at the top stood unchanged. Sorrow and guilt tugged at my heart as I remembered James, the boy who had died there. *If only ...*

I shook off those thoughts, knowing from experience that wishing things had happened differently wouldn't change a thing. I turned toward the walnut desk where my father had spent many days working on ship designs and teaching me everything I knew about sailing. The chair behind the desk beckoned, and I sank into its old leather. This would never be as good as my father's hugs but sitting here made me feel closer to him. My eyes closed trying to hold onto those good memories even as my heart ached at their loss. *I miss you both so much.*

I started to push away from the desk when I noticed the bottom drawer was open. *That's odd. I could have sworn that I'd locked these drawers last time we were here.* I tried to slide the drawer out, but it was stuck. I reached through the opening, feeling for whatever might be blocking the drawer and jerked my hand back when I brushed against something sharp. Blood welled in my palm from a jagged scratch. Putting pressure on the scratch with my other hand, I looked for the box of tissues I had placed on the desk for handling some of the older books, but it was missing. My healing powers would kick in any moment, but I didn't want to make a mess. As if to mock me a drop of blood fell from my clenched hand onto the arm of the chair.

Gold light flashed around the drop of blood like a ripple on the surface of water. *What the hell?* I lifted my injured palm over the arm of the chair and let another drop fall. The same thing happened. Sucking in a breath for courage, I placed my palm down on top of the chair arm. Gold light blazed under my hand. When I lifted my hand away, a glowing seven-pointed sun symbol appeared where there had only been worn brown leather before. The last time I had seen my father's symbol it had been on the wall of this same study, and it had led me to the portal.

The sun symbols seemed to be the key to unlocking secrets my father had hidden in here. I looked again at the arm of the chair and then at the other side. I dug my fingernail into the nearly healed wound on my hand and quickly pressed my palm to the other chair arm. Light blazed and another sun symbol appeared. A breeze swept through the air bringing the scents of the ocean and the sound of seagulls. Across the room, the anchor statue lifted off its base making the clickity-clacking sound of a large anchor on a boat being pulled up.

The sun symbols faded from the chair arms. Cautiously, I crossed the room and peered down into the hole that had been revealed in the base of the anchor statue. A wooden box about the size of a briefcase sat inside. The lid was etched with two names: *Asteri Theophanes* and *Hector Acesius*. Below the names were the symbols for the House of Light and the House of Chaos. Jaxon had found out that my father had changed his name from Hector Acesius to Henry Davies after he left the House of Light. But he had been struggling to find any history on my mother, Stella Theone. Now I knew why. Her real name was Asteri Theophanes. Something about her name tugged at a memory. For a moment, a ruggedly handsome face with eyes shifting into starbursts of color filled my head. His husky Greek-accented voice filled my head. *"You would prefer my human name? I was once called Titan Theophanes."* Was Titan somehow related to my mother?

I pulled the heavy box out with a grunt and set it on the floor. Carefully, I opened the lid. Inside there was a black book with gold lettering that said simply: *For Jillian.* A sad smile tugged at my lips. My mother had always called me Jillian or Jilli-bean. I wished she was here with me now to tell me how to fix this mess with Dia and help me through everything going on. I drew in a deep breath and opened the book. My mother's handwriting filled the page:

Jillian,

We knew that someday we would no longer be able to protect you from our world. We tried so hard to give you a normal life free from persecution and war. If you are reading this, then war has come anyway, and we are no longer able to protect you. Your father and I were never meant to be together. Our families are sworn enemies, but we knew from the moment we met that we had found our other half—our bond-mate. We ran away to be together, and though it was hard, we had each other. When we were blessed with you, it was the happiest day of our lives.

We knew the Chosen mark would draw others to you. We bound your powers, but the gods weren't to be denied. Do you remember the summer you were ten, and how sick you were? Your powers had started to feed on the bindings, and we had to release them. A woman and a small girl came to see us that day. The girl said she heard you calling to her to find you. Claudia King was that girl, and she also bore a Chosen mark. Her mother was as desperate to keep her hidden as we were to protect you.

Together we found a way to lock both of your powers away and hide your marks. We each swore to help protect you girls if the others should find us. We kept you apart to keep your powers from combining to break free, but you found each other again in college. By the time we realized who your friend was, it was too late, the bindings had already started to unravel. Both of your powers had grown too strong to be bound again.

We'd decided to tell you everything when you came home after graduation, but we wanted to leave this for you in case something was to happen. We would take this burden on for you if we could, but the gods have selected you. My visions have shown me pieces of your future, and my heart weeps for all you will endure. Your Chosen will help. Trust in each other, and let nothing separate you. The six of you will be strongest together.

We have gathered what information we could. There are clues and tools left for you to find that will help along the way. You are the key to an ancient prophecy that my brother foretold before he disappeared. Pieces of the original prophecy were hidden amongst the Houses and passed down through the leaders of the guides. Your father was to be one of these leaders, the Kafàli, for the House of Light, but we ran away before he took his vows. We believe that his family knows how to locate the other pieces. They were once a joint House with my guardians and may be willing to help. Gather your Chosen and the pieces of the prophecy. Find my guardians. They know the real history of our people and will help to train you all for what is coming.

Here is the part I was entrusted with:

Six are Chosen.
Of Dark. Of Light.

Our precious girl, there is so much that we should have told you, but know that we only wanted to keep you safe. Perhaps it was selfish of us not to want to share you with our world, but we don't regret one moment of our life with you. We love you so very much, Jilli-bean. No matter what happens remember that and believe in yourself. You are stronger than you know, and our world will need your strength. All of the descendants of the God of Chaos will need your strength.

Love always,

Mom and Dad

Tears tracked down my cheeks unchecked as my fingers traced over the page. Even now my parents were supporting me and guiding me, as they had done my whole life. Another section of my lonely highway crumbled to dust, silencing the thoughts I hadn't even acknowledged. Somewhere in the back of my mind since I learned my parents had been hiding, I had wondered if I had been the reason, and if they had resented me for it. But they hadn't blamed me.

The gods had picked me for a reason. I had no idea why, but it was time to accept my role in this war. No more fumbling in the dark hoping this was a bad dream that would vanish when I woke. Whatever destiny the gods had in store for the Paldimori, I was responsible for helping to shape the final outcome. My parents had given me clues, now it was up to me to put all of the pieces together.

How was I going to be able to do all that needed to be done as both Chosen and Kyrion?

We teleported back to my room in Prometheus only to find a distraught Lydia dabbing at her eyes with a handkerchief, her cheeks ruddy from crying. "Thank the God of Chaos you're back, my lady," she sniffled as Grayson placed the box I had found on the dresser. We both watched as Lydia went still for a moment with that vacant look that said she was talking telepathically. She blinked and informed us, "I've notified the Archai and Kyrion Bennett of your return." Lydia twisted the handkerchief nervously between her fingers. Then the words seemed to burst from her mouth as if she could no longer contain them. "You scared us all going off on your own like that!"

"Lydia, sit down before you faint." I guided her over to the couch in front of the fireplace and helped her to sit down. I looked around for a pitcher of water noticing that more vases of poppies had been placed on the mantle of the fireplace and the table where I had eaten breakfast. Grayson stepped from the bathroom with a glass and handed it to her. "I had Grayson with me. We were completely safe."

"One boy isn't enough protection, my lady," Lydia's face turned pale as she gripped the glass of water tightly. "I'm not supposed to know, but I overheard you talking today, saying you are already bonded to Kyrion Bennett. If you had died, the Kyrion—"

A knock sounded at the door causing Lydia to jump. Water splashed onto her dress but she didn't seem to notice. I took the glass from her trembling hands. She shot to her feet smoothed over her hair and wiped the last of the tears from her cheeks. Then rushed to answer the door before Grayson could get to it.

Selene stepped into the room looking runway ready in a jade-green silk evening gown. She spoke quietly to Lydia, then sent the still pale-faced woman out the door. The clicking of Selene's high heels was the only sound as she walked stiffly across the wooden floor over to my bed. Her fingers trailed over the peach evening gown laying there. "It's a lovely gown, isn't it?" she asked, giving me a deceptively calm smile, the uncharacteristic rigidity of her movements giving away the simmering emotions underneath. "It's from Paris. Did you know that our enemies have nearly taken over all of France? The runner broke his leg trying to avoid capture, but he *did* return with your dress."

"I-I ... No, I didn't know that." The implied accusation in her voice irritated the hell out of me. "Why would you send someone to Paris if it's so dangerous?"

"I wouldn't risk the lives of my people so carelessly," Selene stated with a calm demeanor that was far scarier than if she'd screamed at me. "But an order given by the Kyrion can't be overridden even by me."

"Bennett wouldn't—"

"No, he wouldn't." Selene stated firmly.

Grayson stepped forward to intercede, but I held up my hand. "I don't know what you're accusing me of, but I hate dresses. Why would I send someone to Paris to find some fancy, overpriced ones?"

"I've been asking myself that same question since seeing your note," Selene held out her hand and a familiar-looking piece of stationery with a dancing couple appeared on her palm. "Your pen delivered this to the leader of the runners right after our lesson and the runner was dispatched immediately."

"Click gave you that?" I asked confused by all of this. "That's his stationery, but I didn't write that note. I came back here after our lesson and fell asleep. Then I was with Bennett for training. Besides I don't even know the leader of the runners."

"Guide Athan is in charge of the runners. I believe you met this morning," Selene replied, her tone indicating I was lying my ass off. "In the future, please speak with me before you give orders to the runners. It's my job to make sure our people remain safe. I can't do my job if I am not informed of all decisions."

"I promise I didn't do this, Selene." I pleaded with her to believe me.

"Promises are much more effective when backed by actions, Lia," Selene admonished, and a sick feeling entered my stomach. How many promises had I broken already? "I've rescheduled the coronation planning meeting for the day after tomorrow and given the ladies your apologies. Lydia will assist you with your schedule from now on."

"Damnit, I'm sorry," I said, exasperated with myself for fucking this all up. I had completely forgotten about the plans for this evening in my excitement to make some headway on my quest. I hadn't made a great impression on Selene so far and couldn't blame her for sticking me with a babysitter until I proved myself. "Thanks for taking care of everything. I can see why Bennett leaves you in charge when he's gone." My olive branch froze and shattered under her cold stare. Well, since I was already in hot water I might as well add a log to the fire. "Can we at least talk about this formal dress thing? Shouldn't a Kyrion be able to pick what they want to wear?"

"Kyrion Calidora loved the tradition of formal wear at dinners and meetings," Selene explained, her clasped hands turning white with the effort it was taking to hold that calm composure. Her eyes sparked a challenge as if daring me to contradict her idol. "It's a way of showing respect for our ancestors and those in attendance."

"No offense, but I'm not Calidora," I said as politely as possible. I was never going to measure up to Calidora, but I could still be a good Kyrion. There was a lot of room for change—like that stupid law about outcasts. I could do good here, but not as long as I had to live in the shadow of someone else.

"No, you aren't," Selene responded, her cheeks flushing with indignation. "She would never have left alone in the night with a man not her bond-mate." Her disdain for Grayson was palpable as she scanned over his dark jeans and gray T-shirt. "Nor would she have put Kyrion lives in danger by leaving the House grounds without adequate protection."

"Grayson is my bodyguard—er, themy-something," I replied, my anger starting to grow. Maybe I was more sensitive because of the hell Natalie had put me through with her accusations, but I was damn tired of it. There had been enough accusations thrown my way today. And this one in particular hit a sore spot after my history of cheating boyfriends. I despised cheaters. "I would never cheat on Bennett. Ever. I had something I needed to do, and I knew Grayson could protect me."

Selene turned to Grayson cocking her head. "You've taken the oath of Themis?"

"I have. I am bound to my lady, until my oath is fulfilled." Grayson hooked his thumbs through his belt loops and gave her that boyish smile sure to melt hearts. "Would you like to see my mark, Archai?"

Selene looked startled for a moment before she composed herself and walked closer to him. "If you wouldn't mind."

"It would be my pleasure, lady Archai," Grayson said turning up the charm. He pulled his T-shirt off revealing a sun-kissed bronze chest of lean muscle. His symbol was about three inches tall and set under his right pec. It was the star-like symbol for the House of Chaos but with the exploding colors of a supernova that only my symbol had. Selene seemed mesmerized by either the symbol or his chest as she reached out toward him. Grayson grabbed her hand before she could change her mind and placed it on his chest. "I welcome your touch, *mi flor rara.*"

Selene jerked her hand away as if she had been burned. "I'm not your rare flower." Grayson only smiled wider that she had understood him. She turned to me looking slightly bewildered before donning the Diplomatic Doll face. She waved her hand in Grayson's direction. "I didn't know that he was your Themis. Regardless, he can't be in your room like this. You also can't leave these grounds without permission from Kyrion Bennett." I would have protested but that was likely a direct message from Bennett. It was surprising that he wasn't here yelling it at me himself. "You," Selene pointed at Grayson, "come with me and I'll see if I can find you a tux. Lia, please get dressed for dinner." Then she walked hurriedly out of the room.

"I think I am in love," Grayson whispered beside me.

"She would chew you up and spit you out," I warned him, but he only smiled wider. "Fine, it's your balls that're at risk. Don't say I didn't warn you. Now get out of my room so I can change."

I finally made it down to the dining hall only to find Grayson still in his jeans and T-shirt. The sparkle in his eyes said that whatever had gone down between him and the Diplomatic Doll had been highly entertaining, at least for him. "Where is everyone?" I asked.

"I believe they were given the night off," Grayson said with a mischievous grin. "We have somewhere else to be. Take my hand, my lady."

I opened my mouth to ask more questions, but he grabbed my hand and teleported us away. We landed in a meadow painted in shades of pink under the dying light of the setting sun. I shivered as the cold evening air pierced right through my thin dress but at least it took my mind off the effects the teleporting was having on my stomach. Grayson slipped a robe over my shoulders, and I burrowed into the surprising heat. Snow-capped mountaintops were silhouetted against the pink sky. Piles of snow dotted the trees and the ground around us. I took in a deep breath of the crisp air, feeling freer than I had in weeks now that I was no longer confined indoors.

"What are we doing out here, Yoda-lite?" I asked, making Grayson chuckle at the nickname I had given him.

"Patience, my lady," he said mysteriously. "All good

things come to those who wait. Here let me help you along the trail." He offered me his hand as we stepped around icy patches.

I thanked whoever had bought my shoes that they had gone with flats. Grayson filled me in on some of the history of this place as we made our way across the meadow. The first Chaos descendants to leave Sotirìa had built a small settlement in what we know today as Yellowstone National Park, but the site was attacked soon after. The descendants didn't want to leave the comforting and power-boosting volcanic activity behind, but their enemies had found them. So instead, they moved the entire mountain. The mountain was named Mount Cronos and was relocated to what later became Glacier National Park in Montana. Prometheus was built on the peak of the mountain around 1215 BCE and the whole mountain was hidden from the outside world, much like the island of Sotirìa.

We fell silent after a while, taking in the amazing view. Unfortunately, there was too much on my mind to fully enjoy it. Every mistake I had made since coming here played through my head. Selene had made it look effortless, yet here I was feeling like a kid playing dress up. How could I convince a whole city that I was Kyrion material when I didn't believe it myself? Tomorrow I was going to be introduced as Bennett's bond-mate. The girl that hated being the center of attention was going to be the main focus of this show. I only hoped that I didn't do something stupid. *Please, one of you gods, if you're listening, help me get through the ceremony tomorrow without screwing it up too badly.*

"We are here, my lady," Grayson announced, pulling me from my thoughts.

A stream flowed down the rocky mountainside and around steaming pools of natural hot springs. Groups of tall pine trees dotted the landscape, their branches heavy with the weight of snow. Something tugged at me, drawing me toward the rocky ridge above. I ignored it and stepped up onto one of the rocks lining the largest of the hot springs. "Wow, this place is beautiful. How did you know this was here?"

"I told him," Bennett said stepping from the shadows of the pine trees near a small clearing.

Grayson wished us a good night, then disappeared.

I watched Bennett warily from my spot standing on the rocks. He held out his hand to help me down but I crossed my arms. "Did you bring me out here so no one can hear you yell at me?"

"The thought had crossed my mind," he admitted. "I have been out here for some time."

"Did the cold help calm you?" I asked cautiously.

"Enough to prevent the yelling at least," he wrapped his arms around my waist and lifted me from the rocks. "I had planned to have a picnic with you here this evening, but I find myself reluctant to reward you for such bad behavior today."

"I didn't know I was playing for prizes," I said as I slid down his body until my feet touched the ground. "I'm sorry about leaving without telling anyone. I had this idea and wanted to follow up on it. I'm glad I did because—"

His cool fingers speared into the hair at the nape of my neck pulling my head back so that I had no choice but to look into those dark eyes that were still burning with anger. "Do you have any idea what I went through when your servant could not find you to prepare you for dinner?" His fingers tightened in my hair. "The Talosi have been combing the city looking for you. I was on the verge of sending runners out to see if there were rumors of your kidnapping. Never leave like that again."

His lips crashed down on mine and the bitter taste of his fear filled my senses as I edged the door open to our connection. "Asteràki, I felt the warmth of your presence grow distant but could not reach you. Your mental shields were fully engaged and are the strongest I have ever encountered." He broke away with a growl and nipped at my ear causing my breath to hitch. "I could not even reach the door to our connection to ask for entrance. When will you trust this connection we share to leave the door open to me?"

"One step at a time, wizard boy." I turned my head to rest on his shoulder and he wrapped his arms around my waist. *"Dates first. Then marriage. Then open access to the Lia Channel."* He grunted at my poor attempt at humor, but what could I say? I wasn't trying to punish him for initially trapping me into this bond or trying to use me for my powers. He'd had his reasons just as I had mine now for wanting to take this slow. Trust wasn't easy for me, and everything I'd gone through these last several months had made me even more wary. I had taken the first steps by giving him open access to my powers, the rest would come when I was ready. *"Give me some time to adjust, I haven't had a lifetime of people talking in my head like you have."*

"You are right, wife," he admitted, and I thawed a little more toward him.

The fingers of his other hand trailed along the chain at my neck. Then dipped between my breasts, following the chain until they met the ring hanging there. I leaned back to watch as he slid the ring over the tip of his pointer finger, and it lit up with a crimson color. The ring looked innocent enough as he held it up between us, but nothing in the Paldimori world was ever that simple. He pulled the chain off over my head and slid the ring onto my left ring finger. As soon as it slipped into place, the blue-black mountainous terrain under its smooth surface lit up a turquoise color. Then more colors joined in.

"The ring has never shown more than a color or two in all the time it has been with my family," Bennett said quietly as he rubbed his finger over the ring with a satisfied smile. He was relentless about wanting me to call myself his wife and put his ring back on my finger. "You are the one we have been waiting for, Lia. The ring knows it, and so do I. You doubt yourself because you are still learning your powers and your place in our world. I know your place. It is by my side as we help our people regain our dying powers and rebuild our society to what it once was. Now that you—the Chosen—have joined us nothing is impossible. You only need to believe it for yourself."

A frisson of worry sparked to life inside me at his words, but there was such hope on his face that I couldn't bear to disappoint him. "You're right. I-I'll try harder to believe." I forced a smile and kissed his lips. But his words echoed through my head playing on my doubts: "*Now that you—the Chosen—have joined us nothing is impossible.*" Was I still only a tool to him? The instrument that would be used to defeat his enemies and forge a kingdom of gods? If I joined the ranks of Kyrion would my powers even be my own any longer or just a shared pool from which all six Kyrion could draw strength?

Some hint of my doubts and fears must have leaked through our connection because Bennett sighed and took my hands. "There will never be enough words to tell you how truly sorry I am for bonding with you and not telling you what that meant. For letting Natalie's lies color my judgment of you." He turned my hands over and pressed a kiss into each palm. "But I will spend a lifetime trying to atone. Know that these small hands hold all of my heart."

The doubts and fears melted away as I gripped his hands. "And I will spend a lifetime loving you, Bennett Theo Young."

13

The remains of the picnic were scattered around our blanket nest where we had made love under the stars. I shifted under the blankets, feeling sleepily content after our night spent together here at the hot springs. "You asked about my nickname," Bennett murmured as he kissed my naked shoulder. "It was my mother who called me Bear. She said I growled like a little cub whenever I ate, even as a baby, and had the appetite to match." He pressed our joined hands to my stomach and pulled me even tighter against him. The heat from his naked body pressing into mine chased away the lingering chill from the night air. "Selene was the only other person I would let call me that. We have been friends for a long time. I honestly do not remember a time when she was not hopping around—like the rabbit I named her after— begging Mother for stories and stealing lemon tarts."

"Where was her family?"

"Her mother, Millicent, was the only family she had. No one ever knew who her father was. Mother was an only child with strict parents, as was Millicent. But Millicent had fallen on hard times. I never understood what happened, but Mother must have

saw something in the woman. Father was furious when she moved Millicent into our house. Mother and Millicent became very close friends as their pregnancies progressed. Selene was born two days before me, just down the hall." Bennett was quiet for a moment before he continued, "It is not easy to have friends when you sit on the throne, but not even my father could chase Selene away. Not while my mother still lived anyway."

"I'm glad that you had Selene then," I said, and it was true. There was a part of me that envied Selene's control and confidence, but I would never begrudge their friendship. It eased my mind to know that there had been someone there for the little boy he had been when his mother died. "You don't talk much about your father—"

"There is nothing to talk about," Bennett stated, his body rigid against mine. It seemed we both had our topics that were off-limits: the year I had run away was mine, and his was his father.

"Well, your mother sounds amazing," I replied, thinking of how everyone still revered her even twenty-two years after her death.

"She was a kind and loving person." Bennett sighed against my hair, the tension melting from his body. "But strong in her convictions. She worked hard to bring us technology and open up communications with the outside world. It was thanks to her that we have the runners." He pressed kisses along my neck. "You would have liked her."

Stars gleamed in the clear night sky above us, and I wished on every one of them that there would be more nights like this for us. Time away from the duties and training to just be together. "Is your mother the one who liked poppies? They're all over the room I'm staying in, along with her painting."

"Hmm, I thought Mother's painting and the flowers had been removed from your room," he said. "But yes, she was the one that *loved poppies. You probably noticed them even on the lid of the trunk I gave you. That was my mother's too. It was a wedding gift from her parents."*

"I love that trunk," I gushed, thinking of all the times I had opened and closed the lid to see what would appear. "Thank you for giving it to me and bringing it here. I had forgotten all about it while we were training so hard." At least the trunk mystery was solved. Now if only all the other mysteries in my life could be solved as easily. When the trunk had first shown up in my condo, I had thought maybe Captain Matthews—the pilot who had become one of my friends—had bought it but now I knew that even when we had been at odds, Bennett had been taking care of me. I loved him even more for the thoughtfulness of his gift. "You really do love me to give me a trunk with an unlimited supply of jeans and T-shirts."

"I wanted you to have your own things and feel comfortable in my home. And one day maybe you will call it your home as well." Bennett didn't wait for me to answer before going on to explain, "The power of creation may have been lost to us before we found you, but there are a few among us who can imbed their will into an object to make it perform simple functions such as creating your clothes. Although, I personally prefer you without clothes." Bennett pressed more kisses down my spine. His tongue slipped out to trace along the center of my bond mark. "Mmm, I love this spot here."

I laughed and swatted his thigh. "Behave, you wicked wizard."

He chuckled, his hard chest settling against my back as he wrapped his arm around me once more. "What was it you were asking? Oh yes, Mother loved poppies, and it drove my father crazy that they were all over the house. Sometimes I think that is why she did it. Father once threw an entire platter of bagels out the window because they had poppy seeds on them." Bennett laughed at the memory. "For once, I did not blame him. We had poppy everything when we first started growing them. Now we do not use them as much for ourselves but sell them for their seeds. They make a good profit in the human world. I will take you to the fields one day soon."

I made a humming sound in agreement. It was strange, though, about the poppies and painting in my room. Maybe the servants were confused. The painting was definitely going to have to go. Having Calidora's reflection hovering over me every time I looked in the mirror like she was the benchmark I was to judge myself against was wrecking what little confidence I had managed to find. I had spent years burying everything that was me under my lonely highway. I was trying to be what was expected, but I would never completely bury everything I am again. "I'm a fan of purple and less floral, but I don't want to remove your mother's things."

"My mother is no longer Kyrion here, Lia. You will be." Bennett rolled me onto my back and leaned over to watch me with an imploring look. "This is your home now, and these are your people. The words that you speak become orders that must be obeyed. The decisions you make can mean life or death." I shivered thinking about those people who had died at the tower trying to reach safety within these walls. Regardless of what the law said, weren't they our people too?

"On the day of your coronation, you will pledge to be all things our people need. As Kyrion you will have to make hard decisions." His voice turned gruff with regrets and there was a look of agony on his face as he continued. "There will be times when you will make decisions to protect your people only to find that you hurt those you love more in the end. All I can do is learn from my mistakes so that they are never repeated." His hand

found mine and gripped it tightly as if he was making that a vow to me. He kissed my lips and laid his forehead on mine. "Being Kyrion is not easy, but we will do this together."

"Yes, tog—"

Suddenly, I was falling through darkness. Images flashed past —scenes of death and destruction. The city of Prometheus reduced to a pile of rubble. Bennett lying face down in a pool of blood. Grayson with a sword protruding from his stomach as blood bubbled on his lips. Everyone I knew and loved, dead. I pleaded to make it stop but the scenes flashed by faster and faster.

"Hear me, Chosen," demanded that same female voice that had been taunting me yesterday. "You do not belong here. The gods have set a different course for you. The longer you deny your destiny, the closer our fate draws to destruction." Her voice was filled with heartache as she continued, "My son chose wisely, but your time to be together is not yet come. Find the twin Houses." Her voice began to fade away. "Find the Guardians. Unite the Chosen."

A pair of startling sapphire-blue eyes appeared in the darkness. Bright blue tears fell like rain that soon became a flood that pulled me under. No matter how hard I fought I couldn't find the surface.

I tumbled from the bed gasping for air as the dream reliving our date last night beneath the stars turned into a nightmare. I shoved my hair out of my face and wrapped my arms around myself trying to ward off the cold. My breath misted the air as a bluish-white fog took on a familiar shape near the mirror. Frost formed on the glass, and I nearly bolted for the door when words were written in the ice: *Leave. Save him.* An icy hand brushed down my cheek, and then it was gone.

The room returned to normal temperature, but I was

chilled to the bone. Moonlight spilled across the room perfectly highlighting the painting above the bed. "You're still protecting Bennett aren't you, Calidora? I will too. But I won't leave him. We'll do this together, just like we've promised each other."

I hadn't been able to sleep after my visitor last night and was waiting on Selene when she entered the throne room. We spent the very early morning hours going over more laws. There were laws that dictated what job a person would be assigned based on a ranking system. There were laws that forbid human or non-House of Chaos interaction unless it was sanctioned by the Kyrion, Archai, or Kafàli. Then my least favorite: laws of conduct befitting a Kyrion. During the Games was the only time a Kyrion's days weren't weighed down with upholding some archaic tradition like meditating on a bed of hot coals once a week to strengthen our connection to the God of Chaos. I was half tempted to tell them to send me back into the Games where I could enjoy some freedom and escape the crazy rules.

After my lessons, it was off to my room to get ready for the Bonding Ceremony. I showered, and Lydia curled my hair and pinned it up. The seamstresses had delivered my dress while I was in my lessons and Lydia helped me into the gorgeous gown. The dress had a black halter top and off-the-shoulder bell sleeves. The modified A-line skirt faded from black into a smoky purple and fell to my ankles. Lydia topped it off with a diamond belt and matching dangle earrings with the House of Chaos symbol. And last was a pair of surprisingly comfortable black flats with a matching diamond symbol on the toe. My complaints about wearing a small country's net worth in bling fell on deaf ears.

"You look beautiful, my lady," Lydia exclaimed with a broad smile as I stood in front of the mirror in my bedroom.

"Thank you, Lydia," I replied nervously as I smoothed my hands down the skirt. I finally looked the part of Kyrion but was I ready to become one? I avoided the reflection of Calidora's painting in the mirror and the memory of the words her ghost had spoken. I could do this. Bennett and I would make our bond official today. Then, in less than two weeks, my coronation to become Kyrion and rule by his side would take place. I pressed a hand to my stomach as it tied itself in knots at the thought.

A knock sounded at the door making me jump. "It's time, my lady," Grayson called.

I drew in a ragged breath and let it out slowly. "Coming."

Grayson and three guides I didn't recognize waited in the hallway. They all bowed, then took up position around me as we walked. The house was quiet as we descended the steps to the first floor. "Where is everyone?" I asked, gripping the edges of the wide sleeves in my sweaty hands.

"They are gathering in the town square, my lady," Grayson replied giving me an encouraging grin. "We will meet Kyrion Bennett at the altar where you will declare your intention to bond. Then your people will offer gifts to bless your match, and there will be a celebration."

I nodded, and we continued to the front entrance. I had memorized the words Selene had given me but having a better understanding of what was coming helped to settle my nerves a bit. We proceeded around the circular driveway and down the main cobblestone street. The morning air was surprisingly warm and filled with the smells of baked goods. As we traveled past the first houses, I finally got a glimpse of what life was like in Prometheus, and it was as if we had stepped back in time. The houses were more like small cottages of stone with a chimney and patio. Each had a small yard with stepping-stone walkways and most had flower beds around the house. There were no driveways, power lines for electricity, or vehicles in sight.

We passed a man with his hand wrapped in fire fixing a child's broken wagon by melting the metal axle pieces back together. A woman sold made-to-order muffins from her roadside stand. The ingredients marched themselves through the air, mixed themselves, and then poured themselves into the pan in her hand, where they cooked to perfection in seconds. A group of children shot sparks off the ends of their fingers at each other in a mock battle. A little girl no more than three stood on a patio throwing a temper tantrum and burst into flames from head to toe. Her mother stood with hands on hips talking to the child until she calmed down and the fire went out.

Great, my power outbursts were on par with those of a toddler.

Murmurs started to reach me as we gained attention. "There's Kyrion Bennett's intended bond-mate," an older woman said to her friend as we passed.

"I had hoped we wouldn't see this day," the friend replied solemnly. "At least, not for many more years."

I stumbled, and Grayson caught my hand setting it atop his own. "Are you all right, my lady?" he whispered in an aside, while giving the women a stern look.

I wanted to shout that I was far from ok but a nervous

breakdown was not a good first impression. Instead, I nodded stiffly and removed my hand from his, being sure to step carefully. What had the woman meant? Did they resent my bond with Bennett? Other chatter reached my ears as we entered the more crowded business area of the city, adding to my insecurities. "She isn't what I would have expected from our Kyrion." "I heard she insulted the servants." "We can't lose Kyrion Bennett!" "Maybe they'll wait to complete the bond."

There were a few positive comments grateful Bennett had found a mate, but most were concerned about losing Bennett. Did they think I was going to take him away from them? I had debated all morning on whether I should tell him about the ghostly visit from his mom but had decided it would only hurt him. Instead, I had settled on asking for his help with my quest. Considering the concerns about me taking him away from his people, I now wondered if that was a good idea.

By the time we entered the city square it seemed as if half the population was following us, and the other half was already waiting for us. The Talosi were lined up creating an open path for us as people strained to watch over their shoulders. We walked through one of the Grecian arches that circled the square; beds filled with a variety of flowers in reds and whites dotted the area. At the center of the square was a large white statue of Kyrion Calidora which stood on top of a stone plinth with wide circular steps.

Bennett stood tall and regal in black formal wear at the bottom of the steps. He watched me intently, following my every move as if waiting for me to run. When I stepped up to his side, he held out his hand, and I laid mine on top. My escorts stepped back to join the front of the crowd, and Lydia came forward to remove both of our shoes. When she was done, Bennett turned toward me and said quietly, "I love you, Lia. Nothing and no one will ever change that." The mask of the Kyrion fell away for a moment, and he smiled at me with a look of such love that tears welled in my eyes. "Here before our people I am making our bond official. Our claim on each other cannot be disputed and the world will know that you are mine." He glanced at the people waiting for us to begin the ceremony. "Our people need hope, and for us to show them their Kyrion are united as one.

"We have done everything backwards in this relationship, asteràki," Bennett's voice floated through my head. "Our official 'wedding day' was in a tent on the training grounds during the Games instead of here in our rooms, but I would not change the path that led us here. From this moment forward we will be joined as the God of Chaos intended and rule our people together."

The mask of the Kyrion slipped back into place as Bennett stated loudly, "Jillian Nova Davies, I claim you as my bond-mate."

I licked my dry lips, as a war raged inside me tallying up all of my failures and inadequacies. I wasn't like Selene who was born into this world and could navigate it effortlessly. I would probably never have her calm demeanor and ease with diplomacy. It was going to take me a lifetime to learn all the laws and customs. And clearly the people questioned if this bond was right. I opened my mouth, but nothing came out. Damnit, why was I hesitating? It didn't matter what anyone else thought or how ill-equipped I was for the role. Bennett was the man I loved. The rest would work itself out in time. "Bennett Theo Young, I claim you as my bond-mate."

We stepped up onto the wide ledge of the first step of the

statue base together. "We are born from ash," we chorused loudly.

My hands shook as I waited for whatever was about to happen. The stone beneath us trembled, and suddenly my feet were sinking into ash. The fine silt slid between my toes like the softest sun-warmed sand. We moved up onto the next step and declared, "We are molded in heat."

Hot coals appeared at our feet, and I nearly jumped off the steps. Bennett's rough hand held me steady by his side, and I relaxed when my feet didn't burn. We stepped up onto the top platform. The statue of Bennett's mother loomed over us, blocking out the sun. I looked up at that beautiful face captured forever in white marble wondering what she would have thought of me. Her words from last night echoed through my mind: *My son chose wisely.*

But would she still feel the same if she could see through my bravado to the scared girl underneath? Would she think me unfit for her throne if she saw how little control I had of my powers or how much I had yet to learn about this world? Would she find me a poor match for her son if she knew all those things?

"Mother, I would like for you to meet Lia Davies, my bond-mate." Bennett said quietly with a wistful smile up at the statue. "I think you would have liked each other. Lia is as defiant and stubborn as you were. She will finish the work that you started in changing our world." Bennett glanced at me, those dark eyes filled with love. "You were right, Mother. I chose love over duty, and I do not regret it."

A tear slid down my cheek as I whispered, "I love you too, Bennett."

We raised our joined hands and cried out, "We are bonded in fire."

Fire ringed us on all sides. I jumped in surprise, my

heart galloping in my chest. My power flowed out, reacting with the flames, which shot high into the sky. Bennett looked at me with love and pride dancing in his eyes. For the first time, I craved to say the words I had been denying —to call him my husband. In that moment, I dared to believe we could have it all, and our love would weather anything the gods threw at us.

Bennett doused the flames and turned us to face the crowd. Everyone clapped and a few cheers rang out. I scanned over the faces in the crowd noting that there were many people looking more worried than excited. But it was the pallor upon Christos Athan's face that filled me with foreboding. He was watching Bennett and me with a look of disappointment and regret.

15

We descended the altar and stepped back into our shoes. Selene had now taken control of the crowd with a mastery I was taking notes on. She directed the Talosi to organize the people into a line to greet us and offer their gifts. I noticed Guide Athan more than once by her side preventing problems before they occurred and helping her discreetly. He watched her with awe and—whenever she wasn't looking—something that looked really close to love. Was the old guide secretly in love with the adviser? If so, I would hate to break the news to him that she was married to the job.

When everything was to Selene's satisfaction, she returned to Bennett's side, giving him a nod. Bennett turned to me and announced, "It is tradition for us to ask each other for a gift within our power of granting, and it cannot be denied. What would you ask of me, Lia?"

There were so many things that I could ask for, but there was something that had been weighing heavy on my mind. "I would like for you to remove the law on outcasts so that everyone is welcome here, and no one gets punished for helping them."

Several shocked exclamations rang out from the crowd before they hushed into silence. The pulse in Bennett's jaw ticked, and his lips thinned in displeasure. *"Making such a proclamation without consulting with the other Kyrion will cause chaos. Please, Lia, is there not something else you would ask of me?"*

"I don't want to cause you trouble with the others, but don't they have to listen to you?" I asked, trying to understand how it all worked.

"Yes, I am ruler over all Houses and this decree would be forced upon them," he agreed hesitantly. *"But all Kyrion should have a say; we work best that way. This kind of change should not be undertaken lightly. There are always repercussions to our actions as Kyrion, Lia."*

"I'm sorry I put this on you now, I didn't know how it worked. But I can't condone leaving people helpless when we can do something to change it." I opened the door between us and let him feel my conviction. *"I saw what was on those TV screens. The people who were killed at the tower were only trying to find safety."*

"As you will learn when you become Kyrion, making a decision is easy. It is living with the consequences that is hardest." I got the impression that he knew this all too well. *"It is not always only you who must weather the fallout. Let us hope that neither of us has cause to regret this."*

"My bond-mate has a compassionate heart," Bennett said aloud, with a forced smile. "I, Bennett Theo Young, Kyrion of the House of Chaos, abolish the old law stating that those who will not pledge themselves to a House are considered outcast. All descendants of a House will be afforded protection if they seek it in good faith. Those that seek refuge are subject to all laws and traditions of the House. Furthermore, there will no longer be a penalty for those consorting with outcasts so long as their actions do not betray their House. I so declare this as Lia's Law, and all shall obey."

Bennett had added his own caveats to the law, but I didn't blame him for wanting some degree of assurance that the people they invite in weren't there to cause trouble.

"Thank you, Bennett." I smiled and the crowd gave a weak cheer. "What about your gift?" I opened the door to our connection wider curious about what he could possibly want. *"What would the Kyrion who can command anything ask for?"*

I fidgeted with the sleeves of my dress anxiously waiting for his response. *"I could ask that you leave the connection between us always open,"* he said pensively through our bond. *"But that is something I want you to give freely."* Bennett brushed his hands against my cheek and down my neck to pick up the chain of my necklace. "I ask only that you wear my ring on your finger and never take it off."

"Sneaky, wizard. You finally got your way," I teased. I pulled the ring off the chain and dropped it into his hand. Then said the words my heart had claimed long before I could acknowledge it, "Your wish is granted, husband."

Bennett stilled as he searched my face, his lips slightly parted in awe. "I have been waiting months to hear you claim me as your husband and acknowledge that you are my wife. This gift is even better than I could have asked for. Thank you, my wife." He laughed as he placed the ring on my finger. "My bond-mate drives a hard bargain, but I think we both won this round."

The crowd laughed and cheered more enthusiastically this time. After that a parade of people came before us with their congratulations and gifts. Servants worked diligently to sort through the presents and haul them back to Bennett's house. Their arms were weighed down with silks, brooches, pottery, and more. Other servants set up tables as platter after platter of food was unloaded from a cart. I bumbled my way through the first several introductions, but soon got the hang of the bowing and hand gestures acknowledging their loyalty. My face hurt from smiling and my back was starting to cramp by the time we got through the very long line of well-wishers. Thankfully, we were escorted to a table next and served an array of delicious food. I had very little time for my nerves and doubts, but they lingered there in the background ready to pounce every time I caught a wary look from the crowd.

Music played and performers showed off their fire skills as dinner came to a close. I clapped along with everyone else and made sure to smile through it all. People started to drift off back to their houses or other pursuits about midday. Bennett was called away to address an issue and Selene was busy directing the clean-up. I sat alone at the table with Grayson and the three guides who had apparently been assigned to me, all of them standing at my back like stone pillars. I drew aimless patterns in the remains of my choco-late cake as the dwindling groups of people chatted and laughed. I felt like the mismatched piece in a puzzle that hadn't yet found my true place. I had kept to myself in Port Lawson, and in Sotiria I had discovered I was the first Chosen. Here I was an outsider: an unknown raised by the hated humans and ignorant of the Paldimori ways.

This was my wedding day, and I had never felt more alone. My best friend hadn't been here to help me get ready and gush over this dress. My husband hadn't shoved cake in my face or held me close on the dance floor as we had our first dance as a married couple. My parents weren't here to walk me down the aisle or cry over my ring. With everything going on, I hadn't thought about what this day really meant for me until this moment. The realization that I would never have the traditional wedding that I had once dreamed of as a little girl had me choking back tears.

I miss you Mom and Dad. I miss you Dia.

Bennett came back a half hour later and said he had someone he wanted me to meet. We walked down a side street escorted by Grayson and several guides. A two-story stone building sat at the end of the street bearing a weathered wooden shop sign painted with a crossed sword and axe that said simply: *Mark's.* Four guides preceded us into the dimly lit interior and fanned out around the shop, checking everything over. My flats scuffed over the stone floor as we made our way into what looked like a cosplayer's wet dream. Suits of armor stood to attention on a balcony above the front desk, while the tables in the central part of the room were piled with sturdy leather vests, boots, and various other battle gear. Different types of weapons featured in the lighted alcoves lining each wall, and the smell of leather and gunpowder tickled my nose.

A dark-skinned giant of a man with a bald head stood in front of the desk watching silently as we approached. He wore a leather vest, which opened to reveal folds of scars marring his chest and traveling up to his left cheek to pull down the corner of his mouth as he smiled. He bowed and addressed Bennett and me in a raspy voice. "My Lord and Lady Kyrion. I am humbled to have you in my shop."

"Lia, I would like you to meet our weapons-master, Mark Harris." Bennett nodded to the man fondly. "Mark is Devon Harris's brother. And he wanted to meet you."

The guides and Grayson stayed discreetly in the background as Mark congratulated us and we chatted. To my surprise, I found myself liking the soft-spoken man far better than his gruff younger brother, Devon, who was Bennett's Kafàli. Mark was one of the few people in this city who welcomed me without furtive glances or looks of mistrust.

There was also something about his shop that drew me. I wanted to wander around, but those damn traditions had to be observed. Mark presented us with another gift: a pair of daggers with blood-red handles inlaid with a black House of Chaos symbol. In my opinion, they were the best gift we had received, and I told Mark this. Apparently, that was a major insult to the other gift-givers based on the tightening of Bennett's hand on mine and his attempt to explain my lack of knowledge of the customs. Mark laughed it off, and I liked him even more for that.

We said our goodbyes and walked back to Bennett's house with our company of escorts. The whole way there I debated how to broach the subject that I needed to discuss. I never got the chance. Guide Athan was waiting for us looking graver than ever as soon as we entered the house. Bennett turned to me with a look of apology, but I nudged him forward. He was needed, and I wanted to get the hell out of this dress. Besides, it wasn't like we could rush off to a deserted island honeymoon and play naked Twister in the sand for a few weeks. I still had to make it through the coronation.

My retinue surrounded me as I made my way to my room deep in thought. The answers I needed to find the twin Houses were out there, and I had a good idea on where to start. I wanted Bennett to come with me so that we could do this together, but would he?

"Penny for your thoughts, my lady," Grayson said as he opened the door to my room.

"I'm not sure a penny would cover the cost on these

thoughts, my friend." I shook off the melancholy mood and gave him a smile. "It's nothing, Grayson."

"Kyrion Bennett asked me to train with you this afternoon, my lady." Grayson gave me his boyish smile as he leaned forward so only I could hear him. "I have an idea that might take your mind off of such heavy thoughts. Let me know when you are ready."

I gave him a nod and entered my room to find Lydia waiting for me. She helped me change out of the dress, and I gave her some new stipulations to our arrangement. She wasn't to help me dress anymore except for formal wear, and I would be wearing jeans unless there was some event that necessitated a dress. Lydia tidied the room with jerky movements, clearly upset that I wasn't following in the footsteps of Kyrion Calidora. I was just happy to have the bathroom to myself to change and did a little happy dance after I slipped back into my jeans.

I left Lydia to her work and joined Grayson in the hall. "Brace yourself, my lady," he whispered shielding us from the guides standing on either side of my door as we linked arms. "We are going to teleport."

"What about them?" I whispered back, nodding in the guides' direction.

"You are now the official bond-mate to the Kyrion, my lady. Give them an order."

This giving orders thing was something I would have to get used to. "Hey boys, we're off to do some training. Uh, go do what you would normally do and don't disturb us."

"My lady, has the Kyrion—" one of the guides started to protest.

I clutched Grayson tighter and shouted, "Beam me up, Scotty!" Then we disappeared from the hallway.

16

Grayson and I landed in the meadow near the hot springs. Axol came bounding up to give us both a sniff. I scratched the dog behind the ears, and he gave my hand a lick, making me laugh. Grayson had been right: this was exactly what I needed. Click flew through the air and danced around my head. I gave him a quick pat too before he flew off. Axol barked as the gold pen zipped through the air way above his head. Click swooped down right in front of the dog's nose, taunting him, and barely missed becoming dog kibble. I could warn him about all those sharp teeth, but I doubted it would do any good given Click's stubborn streak.

Axol hunched down preparing to pounce on Click who had stopped to draw in the snow. "Axol, no!" I shouted but the dog ignored me, intent on his prey. I quickly ran over and grabbed the dog's collar and grunted out, "Looks like I'm going to have to figure how this command stuff works for both people and dogs. No, Axol, Click is not a doggie treat."

Grayson said something in Greek, and Axol obediently sat. Damn it, I was also going to have to learn to speak the language. Grayson turned toward me with a look of complete faith. "You will be co-ruler here, my lady. You are Chosen. It is you who will shape our world into what we are to become."

Who was I to shape a whole world? The broken pavement of my lonely highway flashed through my mind. The pavement was cracked and crumbling, but it wasn't completely destroyed yet. Forgiving myself for not being able to save my parents had been the first step. The screams of my mother and the sound of the raging water that had taken them from me had faded. But there were nightmares still buried there that haunted me. Memories from that year I had run away to live on the streets. All of the things that had happened during the Games that there hadn't really been time to deal with. They all lurked there in the cavernous space beneath the highway, waiting to ambush me. I doubted I would ever truly be free of my nightmares, but I was going to find answers that might help alleviate them.

The young servant girl with the blue-tinted hair now appeared in the meadow and bowed in my direction. "Come," Grayson said, "she will watch Axol and Click."

I made a neutral humming sound, watching the girl toss a stick for Axol. There was something about her that seemed different than the other people I had met here. I just couldn't put my finger on what it was. Grayson nudged me toward the path, and we walked toward the hot springs in silence.

"There are some volcanic vents beyond the ridge." Grayson pointed to the rocky peak up the mountain from where we stood. "We may be close enough for you to use that energy to help in controlling your powers."

"Are you saying we should train now? Cuz I thought I was going to get to relax in this hot spring."

"You will be Kyrion here soon." Grayson watched me closely. "The people here will come to rely on you to help them settle grievances and to allay their fears that our enemies will never breach the city walls. Can you be sure that *you* will not be a threat to them if your powers are not controlled?"

"Shit, no rest for the weary, I guess."

Grayson nodded, his bright hazel eyes full of understanding: *Adulting sucks.*

"Fine. Let's train."

Grayson took up position about forty yards further up the side of the mountain next to a small group of pine trees well out of the line of fire. "Concentrate, my lady. Let the power flow up from your center and into your hand," he advised.

It was a struggle to focus with the tempting warmth that radiated from the hot spring right in front of me. All I really wanted to do was to sink into the warm water and let it wash away my burdens.

Fine, work first, then relaxation. Here goes.

I closed my eyes and sought out my powers. The bright ball of light at my center welcomed me like a long-lost friend. Slowly, I coaxed out a bit of the power, pulling it through my body until my hand tingled. I opened my eyes to find a flame no more than an inch high, flickering weakly on my upturned palm. I pulled on more power, feeding it to the flame.

"That's it, my lady. Keep the power flowing steadily." Grayson's boyish grin was back and as infectious as ever. My lips curled up in a proud smile. I was controlling it all on my own. Bennett's harsh training method really had worked.

"When you are ready, release the flame at that rock over there." Grayson pointed to a large rock about ten yards away and demonstrated the motion he wanted me to perform. He pulled his hand back toward his chest, palm facing the rock, and then pushed his palm out quickly in front of him. Messy black curls flopped onto his forehead at the quick movement. "Now you try, my lady."

I followed his directions exactly, but when it came time to launch my fire at the target it snuffed out. I tried again but got the same results. Over and over again, the same thing happened. I ground my teeth in frustration with each failure. Some great Chosen one I was turning out to be. Hours later the most I had accomplished was to make the flame fall off my palm into the hot springs. Anger built in my chest and the flow of power pushed into the flame with such force that a ball of fire completely engulfed my hand. Grayson yelled something, but I was too focused on trying to keep on top of this bucking bronco as my powers came pouring out of me.

Before I could direct the ball of flame toward a target, it launched from my palm. The fireball took a crazy swooping path through the air. Grayson dropped to the ground, barely avoiding getting hit. The fireball smacked into a boulder near the top of the ridge, and it seemed as if half the mountain exploded. A landslide of dirt and rocks tumbled down. Trees were toppled. Dust clouds filled the sky. Water shot into the air as rocks hit the stream. Grayson jumped to his feet and ran toward me shouting. His voice was drowned out by the angry rumbling of rock and debris as it barreled toward us. I jumped along the rocks as fast as I could, hoping to reach Grayson in time. What I would do when I got to him, I had no clue, but this was my fault. No way was he getting hurt because of me.

One minute, I was leaping to another rock. The next, a strong arm wrapped around my waist to spin me around and crush me against a hard chest. Bennett's smoky toasted almond scent filled my nose, and I dropped the fist that had been aimed at his head. I twisted in his arms trying to see what was happening. "We have to help Grayson!"

"Stay still," Bennett ordered. The protest died on my tongue as a wave of his power surged out toward the landslide. The grumbling sound tapered off almost immediately. The landslide was frozen like a giant dark wall threatening to crush us. Bennett painstakingly re-directed the dirt, rocks, and debris to the other side of the ridge where it wouldn't cause any damage. His body was a tense immovable force surrounding me until the last of the landslide was cleared away. Axol's barking broke the tense silence. The dog eagerly nudged against Bennett's leg seeking attention. The servant who had been watching them was nowhere in sight. Click took a page from the dog's book and started nudging me too. But I ignored him as my eyes anxiously scanned the destroyed mountainside for Grayson.

A choked cough sounded from a dusty pile lying a few yards away. I pushed out of Bennett's arms and went over to kneel next to Grayson. Dirt and bits of pine needles slid to the ground as I helped him to his feet. Grayson bent at the waist, as a coughing fit hit. I went a little light-headed in sheer relief and sank down to sit on the rocks.

"M-my lady, are you ok?" Grayson kneeled beside me, his dirt-streaked face lined with worry.

"I should be asking you that. God, I'm so sorry." I grabbed him in a bone-cracking hug. My face was mashed tight against his shoulder, tears leaving tracks along his black T-shirt. "I almost killed us both, Grayson. I can't do this. I can't be this thing—this ... Chosen."

"Lia," Bennett said as he stroked my back. "We have lived with the knowledge of our powers since we were young. We have had many years of training. You have only just awakened your powers and started to learn them. Give yourself time."

I pulled away from Grayson and turned to look at Bennett. "There is no time. Don't you feel it?" My fist clenched against my stomach where fear and guilt were once again threatening to force my powers to pour out of me. That incessant nagging in the back of my mind sounded like the odd chiming of the Moirai: *thump-thump, thump-thump, whir, tickety-tock.* "The Chosen, the prophecy, my quest, the Games. It's all tied together somehow. And time is running out for all of us."

"What are you saying, Lia?" Bennett asked cautiously.

"I'm saying that I need to start looking for answers, and I know where we need to go."

"And where would that be?" he said with a resigned sigh as if he already knew.

"The House of Light," I stated as I squared my shoulders ready for a fight. "I want you to take me to meet my father's people."

17

A stucco wall badly in need of patching appeared only inches from my nose as we materialized in Sicily. I stumbled forward and barely managed to save my face from smashing into the wall. Bennett's firm grip settled on my waist, steadying me as I adjusted to my cells being rearranged from teleporting back into a me-shape. It had taken less convincing than I had expected to get Bennett to agree to this trip, and I didn't know if I should be concerned about that or not. I looked around. Lights over metal garage doors spaced tightly under a row of small balconies lined a narrow alley. The windows above us were dark, and the sound of the ocean waves filled the early morning air. Overhead, the sky still twinkled with a thousand stars.

"Where are we?" I whispered, patting my hip holster to make sure Click was still there. I had instructed him to play the part of a regular ink pen unless I gave him a signal.

"Mazara del Vallo. A town in the province of Trapani in southwestern Sicily." Bennett cocked his head as if listening for something, then pointed to our left. Grayson took off in that direction as several guides spread out around us.

Bennett nudged me in front of him, and we followed Grayson. "This town is well known for its fishing," Bennett said. "It is likely why your father went into shipbuilding. He would have been very comfortable on the water having grown up here."

"How did you know where to find my father's family?"

"Jaxon is brilliant at many things." Bennett pulled me to a stop when we came to an intersection. A few moments of silence passed before he nudged me to the left, and we moved on. "He would deny that, of course. My stepbrother credits me with far too much and himself with far too little. The truth is, without Jaxon we would never have accomplished all that we have since I took over as ruler. He is more than our lawyer and my ally amongst the other Kyrion. He has shored up all of our finances and diversified our holdings, ensuring that we have our hands in every industry in the human world. He has single-handedly found more Potentials for the Games than ever before. All by embracing technology, which our Houses have fought against for so long. Without him, we would never have been able to find another contestant at such short notice to take your place."

I cringed away from any thoughts of the Games and the fact that it was Dia who was taking my place. Dia and I had both made our decisions. There was no going back. My only hope was that she would be safe, and that we would be able to fix this rift between us.

We were silent after that, stealthily weaving our way through alley after alley in what seemed like an endless maze.

Finally, we arrived in a piazza. Antique lanterns cast their light across the square reflecting off a golden sun symbol at the center. We stayed near the side of the buildings, making our way to the tall church at the other end of the square fronted by large palm trees, towers spearing into the sky at each corner. The second-story parapet was lined with statues of angels and demons in battle. On the third floor, a large relief sculpture showed a cross being lifted between two angels toward a golden sun symbol.

"These guys aren't subtle at all," I said, motioning toward the artwork.

"The God of Chaos and the human's God are brothers of a sort. But only someone of our world would know the symbols are more than decoration." Bennett studied the symbols with a predatory intensity that sent a shiver down my spine. Seeing him like this, there was no doubt that he had done his fair share to protect his people no matter what he said. Jaxon may be the brains, but Bennett was the fierce leader and warrior that his people followed without question.

"To put both the cross and the sun on their home base is unusual. They either have an odd sense of humor, or they are honoring both gods outright," Bennett mused. "There is more here than is seen at first glance. Light is, at its very basis, a frequency that can be manipulated. Look deeper and tell me what you see."

I reached down deep to that ball of light at my center and teased out a tiny tendril of power. Breath rushed from my lungs as a whole other world slowly revealed itself. A skyscraper—lit up like a neon Christmas tree—sat on top of the church. Glowing walkways branched off in all directions. I turned in a circle to see an entire neon city sitting atop the human town we had traveled through to get here.

"I had heard of the City of Light, but never thought to see it for myself. They are supposedly the most technologically advanced of all Houses," Grayson whispered in awe. "But how do we get in?"

"That is where I can help," a voice rasped in English with a heavy Italian accent from the dark archway of the church. The guides had their swords out ready to attack if needed. A man who could have passed for Robert De Niro's brother stepped into the lantern light. His white robes covered him from neck to toe, but his muscular frame was still evident. Gray shoulder-length hair framed his face. My powers clamored inside me, torn between wanting to reach out to greet him, or to strike him down. I smoothed my hand over the rolling ball of light at my center and smiled as it calmed enough for me to stay in control.

Faded brown eyes met mine not missing a thing. "My name is Giovanni Acesius," the man said. "Welcome to the House of Light, granddaughter."

18

Grayson and I followed the old man silently. There were so many questions spinning around in my head I was surprised I was able to walk at all. Why was my grandfather welcoming us to his House when we were enemies? Was this a trap? Bennett hadn't seemed surprised by any of this and spoke quietly to the guides near the entrance of the church. What did he know and why hadn't he told me?

It was like tugging at a giant ball of yarn: every time I unraveled one secret, there was another one right behind it.

Empty rows of pews stretched out on either side of us. Murals depicting battling angels and demons lined every wall and the tall ceiling above us. Even the pulpit was adorned with pictures of angelic wars. Then, when my eyes adjusted, I saw that every scene was actually showing battles of the descendants of the gods. Familiar House symbols—and many I had never seen before—marked each figure. In one mural, fire twisted around the throat of a woman like a snake, while her opponent was riddled with shards of ice. On and on it went. It was odd seeing the world with this dual vision—the angels and demons that those without power would see, and what I, as Paldimori, knew was really there.

"History is not to be forgotten," Giovanni said quietly.

I hadn't realized I had stopped walking. He watched me closely as if judging my reaction. "Is that what the paintings are? Your history?"

"Our history. Our future," he said ambiguously, the lines that age had carved into his face deepening with sadness. "They are often the same."

"Those who do not learn from history are destined to repeat it?" I asked, repeating the old philosopher's adage. "I can't get on board with that. I'm a forge-your-own-path kinda girl."

"You are your father's daughter in this." Giovanni's wrinkled hand rested on my shoulder. My first reaction was to push him away, but his kind eyes were radiating a sadness I knew all too well. The scent of the ocean and fresh sheets hit me as he leaned closer. For a moment, I could see my father in this stranger, and I wanted to grasp onto this last piece of him.

"His path took him far from his past," Giovanni said. "Yet you are here. Some say all roads lead home."

Molly had once told me that the Houses tried to keep their lines pure. If my father had married outside of his House, it would have been frowned upon, but I hadn't gotten the impression it was strictly forbidden. My father believed in duty and honor. He had been days away from becoming the next Kafàli here. Yet he had turned his back on everything he knew to run away with my mother. Father had loved her so much that he would have married her no matter what anyone said. So why run away? Was there something else happening here in this House that drove him to run?

"This isn't my home," I said, not wanting to offend the man, but making it clear that I had no obligations here. I may have inherited my father's nose and some part of his powers, but that would never make me part of this House. Technologically advanced or not, this place still screamed that they took their rules and traditions very seriously. Very much like another House which was currently training me in all their own stuffy traditions. Which begged the question why was I letting them make me into another version of Calidora? My temperament was much closer to my mother's, and she would never have let others dictate her life for her or stifle her with rules. Things were going to have to change when we returned to Prometheus.

The more immediate question was what I wanted from this visit. I hadn't come here seeking out a family connection, but would it be so bad to hear my grandfather's side of the story? Would my father have wanted that? Whatever had driven my father to run, I wasn't going to belittle his choices by blindly jumping on the House of Light bandwagon. I wanted answers and the only way to get them was to be open to hearing what these people had to say.

Giovanni nodded in understanding. "Please excuse an old man for meddling. When you are my age, life is too short for holding your tongue. But I would very much like to teach you about your father and our family."

"There's nothing that you need to ask my forgiveness for," I reassured him. My father may have been another story, but Giovanni would have to work that out for himself. A pang of longing hit me. It was there every single time I talked about my parents, but it was getting easier the more I remembered the good times. "You lost your son. I lost my father. He was a good man who died protecting the people he loved. Maybe ... would you like me to tell you about him some time?"

"Sí, you would bless this old man with a great gift." He squeezed my hand. "Now we go. Jameson is not so patient."

We joined Bennett and Grayson by the confessionals. The guides had spread out around the church but didn't appear to be coming with us. Giovanni opened the door to the middle booth and gestured for us to enter. Bennett and Grayson pressed close on either side of me, their bodies taunt with tension and their eyes alert, taking in everything. Mahogany walls lined all four sides of a space that was much bigger than its exterior would lead you to believe. Giovanni closed the door and pressed his hand to a panel in its center. Bright light filled the booth, and the wooden walls melted away to reveal a sleek metal elevator with a panel displaying dozens of buttons. The old man selected the top floor, and we shot upward.

"*How long have you known my grandfather?*" I asked Bennett.

"*I have never met him personally until now. When Jaxon investigated your father, he crossed paths with Giovanni here at the local library. It seems the two share a love of knowledge.*"

Bennett's hand settled on my lower back, his thumb stroking it soothingly. I relaxed slightly, and my flaring powers followed suit. Setting the building on fire would not be a great opening for a we-come-in-peace meeting.

"*Jaxon tested the waters to determine what kind of family reunion your father would have received. Your grandfather is a very smart man. Do not let the robes and old-man talk fool you. He is still the Kafàli here. Unlike most Houses, the House of Light has fully embraced the twenty-first century and taken it even further by combining their powers with technology. With the little information Jaxon gave away, Giovanni learned of your existence and tracked you to Mercer Island. That was one of the reasons for moving you to Sotirìa. We were not sure of his intentions until a few days ago, when he requested to meet you."*

"When were you planning to tell me this?" I asked bitterly. Everything with the Paldimori felt like a chess game, and I was the clueless pawn. Pawns were usually the first to be sacrificed, and I was damn tired of being left in the dark waiting for the axe to fall. It was time to call my own shots. "What does he want?"

"I would have told you as soon as I could ensure your safety. You pushed the timetable up, so now we wait to see what his intentions are. His response to our missive claims he only wants to get to know you and for you to learn about your father's House." Bennett's hand pressed tightly against my back as if he were seconds from yanking me out of here. His voice rumbled through our connection, *"I had suggested that we meet to form an agreement between our two Houses. He has refused all of my offers unless you are part of the meeting. I have no doubt he will ask you to stay here."*

"He already did," I replied drily. Bennett was about to go supernova if the manic tic in his jaw was any indication. Welcome to my anger-management program—lots of anger, very little management. Now he knew how it felt to be out of the loop. I wanted to leave him hanging, wondering what I had decided, but I wasn't a petty asshole. *"Relax, wizard boy. I'm not planning on vacationing here in the City of Oz."*

Out of the corner of my eye, I noticed the rigid tension in his shoulders lessen as the firm pressure of his palm on my back eased. The elevator doors opened, and Grayson moved first. Bennett nudged me forward, keeping me between him and Grayson, as we stepped into a room straight out of a sci-fi movie. Everything was white and sterile-looking. A webbing of honeycomb-shaped windows domed the entire top floor. Twelve wave loungers formed a circle at the center of the room. Hanging from the ceiling at their center was a multi-sided Jumbotron video display—like they use in stadiums. The only color came from the neon city beyond the windows that stretched out along the coastline far below.

Bennett and I halted beside a console covered in buttons. Grayson took up a stance a few steps behind my right shoulder, looking laid-back, but his eyes constantly scanning the room. So much stark white everywhere could explain why I missed seeing the other person in the room until he rose from one of the loungers. Hooded white robes vanished to reveal a man who looked to be a few years younger than me. The term "fallen angel" came to mind as I stared at him. He was so gorgeous that he may have even surpassed Jaxon's good looks—not that I would ever tell the descendant of Eros that. The new guy's blonde hair was spiked in a fauxhawk. His hazel eyes were alight with an inner fire that burned with embers of gold. He wore faded jeans and a Han Solo T-shirt molded to a muscular frame.

Ordinarily, I would judge him as good people since he was a Star Wars fan, but my instincts were saying something different. My skin buzzed as if I was covered in fire ants, and my gut reaction was to throw a fireball at his beautiful face. Bennett gripped my wrist. When had I fallen into a fighting stance?

"Show me your mark, Chosen," the man ordered without preamble.

"Youth today are so impatient," Giovanni tutted. "This is Jameson Parisi, Kyrion Apollo of the House of Light. Can we not have our guests sit before you start making demands, Jameson? Perhaps a drink first?"

"I am leader of this House. I will make the decisions on how to welcome our guests," Jameson said arrogantly in perfect English. "We have been neutral in the war for eight years. Yet you want us to risk everything we have built—the peace my father died to give us—for silly fairy tales. I agreed to this meeting out of respect for you, Giovanni, but I can't afford for my judgment to be clouded by family ties. If she really is Chosen, then she'll prove it."

I stepped forward before Giovanni could reply, Grayson joining me.

"I'm not a circus act, asshole."

"We have agreed to offer you proof," Bennett stated in that hard voice of Kyrion Chaos. He stepped forward to grab my wrist as if he were holding me back from doing something stupid. He was getting to know my reactions well, but if he was *really* smart, he wouldn't have made this deal without me. My fists clenched. We seemed to always come back to this point—where he was making decisions, and I was left to deal with them when they came to light. Anger and hurt mixed together in a dangerous combination that threatened my control.

If only freakin' laser beams could shoot out of my eyes there would be toasted Kyrion all over the room. As if my powers agreed, they filled my body, ready for action. *Whoa! That was only a figure of speech; we don't really want to hurt anyone.* To my surprise my powers listened and settled down.

I tuned back into the conversation to hear Bennett say, "You are in no position to make demands." Bennett held out his hand and a gun appeared on his palm. It had a matte gray grip and the clear barrel was filled with a glowing gold liquid. "You say your House is neutral, yet this very advanced weapon was found in the remains of Chaméni Elpída. My people witnessed only soldiers belonging to the House of Water and the House of Flames in the battle. Oh and Paden, of course, from the House of Spirits. What is it you really want?"

"Very good," Jameson said as the anger radiating off of him only moments ago was replaced with smug satisfaction. The man was more mercurial than me during PMS. "I knew you wouldn't be able to stall meeting with me any longer once you found my calling card." Jameson gestured to the gun. "A nice bit of technology that we've developed, don't you think? Paden has only one obsession—his daughter. When little birdies whispered to me that he'd begun a frantic search for her once again it didn't take much to figure out his next move." Jameson snapped his fingers and a tumbler of amber colored liquor slid into his hand. He sipped the drink watching Bennett's irritation build. "A fine Disoronno. Care for some?"

"What game are you playing, Apollo?" Bennett bit out, clearly pissed about being manipulated.

"I happen to like chess," Jameson quipped and tossed back the rest of his drink. "Chess is a game of strategy and careful maneuvering to position your opponent where you want them to be. And then bam!"—he threw the tumbler down, and glass shards scattered across the floor—"you deliver the death blow before they ever see it coming. My father was a good man. An honest man, that wanted only for our people to be left in peace." Sadness flickered across his face before his gaze turned cold. "I'm not my father. There is only one way peace has ever been achieved, and that's by force. I've done what I can from the shadows." He held out his hand and the gun floated over to him. "It's time to come into the light." Jameson teleported, and I gulped as the barrel of the gun slid along my cheek. "All we've been missing on this gameboard is the queen."

Bennett grabbed my arm, spinning me away from the gun, and I stumbled into the console. Grayson wrestled the gun away from Jameson who teleported back across the room and braced himself against a lounger as he laughed his ass off. All of the neon lights in this city must have fried his brain cells.

I straightened from the console and gripped Bennett's wrist before he could launch himself at Kyrion Crayzpants. What had Jameson meant about me being the missing game piece? Did he know something about the prophesy?

Giovanni stepped into the middle of the room, sweeping his hand out to make the broken glass disappear before he turned to us with a pleading look. "Calm, Kyrion Chaos. There is no danger here. Jameson has never outgrown his poor taste in fashion, nor his flair for drama."

Bennett vibrated with anger. "If he touches my bond-mate again, you will be searching for a new Kyrion."

Giovanni nodded. "My apologies." He turned toward the still laughing man. "Jameson, this is no time for tricks!"

"Yes, yes," Jameson said sweeping a mocking bow in our direction. "Just a bit of fun. Sorry to have alarmed you."

Giovanni sighed, "You are here because we want true peace. Allow my granddaughter to come here to learn of her heritage. Let us train her in the light that I can see within her. In exchange, we will form a truce with the House of Chaos."

Hold up, were they trying to make arrangements about *me* without my vote again? All of this alpha male control-freak crap was going to change. "You can't just—"

Jameson teleported across the room to stand next

Giovanni. All traces of humor were gone as his voice dropped into a low rumble filled with a dark hatred that had me holding tighter to Bennett's wrist. "Agree to give us access to the Chosen, and we will fight beside you. We will help you rip those who have taken so much from us from this world and send them back in pieces to the gods that they betrayed."

Bennett's other hand settled over mine in reassurance. "I will agree to this truce, but Lia will visit here only when she wants and never alone."

Ahh shit, guess I'll be spending time here after all. These House of Light jerkwads had better not say one bad thing about my father or there was going to be hell to pay.

Giovanni nodded to Jameson, who said, "It's agreed. From this moment the House of Light and the House of Chaos are allies." Bennett released me and held his hand up. A stream of black light shot out toward the two House of Light men still standing several feet away. A shout stuck in my throat as a golden stream of light shot out from Jameson's hand at the same time. The two lights clashed together in a shower of sparks, but instead of exploding, the tiniest tendril of each power wove together in an intricate knot. Then they cut off abruptly.

"Our truce is sealed," Jameson said. "You have my power signature and can reach me telepathically if needed. Our people may have felt the change through their connection to their Kyrion, but make no mistake, the compulsion is still there. Your Chosen is feeling it even now. I hope for the sake of this truce, your people can overcome the urge to kill us."

The cold, emotionless mask of Kyrion Chaos stared down the man as if he was an insignificant bug. "We will honor the truce. Make sure your people do the same. Other than proof of her standing, Lia is off-limits to you. Do not speak of her again." Bennett turned toward me his face softening only slightly. "Grayson and I will shield you from their view, Lia. You need only raise the back of your shirt. The mark has changed even since you were claimed. Kyrion Apollo is familiar with the House of Chaos symbol and will realize your mark is much more."

One more thing he had forgotten to mention.

"Dammit, Bennett." My voice quivered with a mixture of anger and hurt. *"When were you going to tell me about any of this?"*

"The House of Light observes some of the old customs still when dealing with other Houses. To bare our marks in meetings is one of them." Bennett's strained voice cut through the red haze that was threatening to edge out my reason. He wasn't enjoying this either. *"I did not want you to dread this the whole way here. I hate that he will see one ounce of your skin that should be for my eyes only."*

"But what compulsion is he talking about?" I asked, not realizing I had said that out loud.

"Little supposed Chosen, you have much to learn." Jameson chuckled, drawing my attention away from Bennett. "Long ago there was a war between Houses and one of our ancestors used a power called Voice on all of our people. It's a very dangerous power because with it, you can compel anyone to do what you want regardless of their will. Our ancestor used this power during a moment of grief and anger to declare all of the opposing Houses as traitors to be cut down whenever they encountered each other. The compulsion has weakened over time, but those instincts you have been fighting to lash out at us are from that command. For his actions, the ancestor's name has been stricken from our history books and the use of Voice forbidden to all."

Jameson's face tightened with anger. "All this time later, we're still fighting each other."

"Do not blame the compulsion for the acts your people have committed." Bennett's fingers dug into my wrist so hard they were sure to leave a bruise. His rage was a palpable force dominating the room. Grayson stiffened beside me, giving Bennett a sharp look of disapproval. Bennett's grip loosened, and he rubbed his thumb over the sore spot.

"Your kind still want what you have always wanted," Bennett snarled. "To eliminate us and take over the world. Do not try to pretty it up with your half-truths. The twelve Houses betrayed our gods. They are the reason neither side has known peace."

"My House is not to blame," Jameson gritted out, his face flushed red and a vein standing out on his forehead, his own anger pushing back until the whole room felt on the verge of erupting. He took an aggressive step forward, but Giovanni placed his hand on his shoulder, halting him.

"You know nothing. My family has never agreed with the annihilation of the Chaonians or Paldimori or whatever you're calling yourselves now. My father worked hard to find a way to break the compulsion and end this madness," Jameson spat, vibrating with anger and pain. "And he was killed for it. We have suffered on both sides. Make no mistake—I will protect my people from any threat, truce or not."

"Ok boys, let's just settle down," I said. "No need to undo all that truce stuff, already." Before either could continue their "I have more right to be pissed than you do" battle, I spun around and yanked my shirt off. Standing there in my bra, I was keenly aware of all the eyes on me. Nothing like a topless woman to break up a pissing match.

I glanced over my shoulder to find Giovanni and Jameson studying my symbol with a look of awe. Grayson stepped between us, blocking their view. Bennett grabbed my shirt off the floor and stuffed me back into it. "Do not look at her," he commanded harshly.

"*Asteràki, are you trying to get the pretty boy Kyrion and your grandfather killed?*" Bennett growled at me. "*Never bare yourself like that to anyone other than me again, or we will see how that lovely backside of yours looks with my handprints upon it.*"

An image of Bennett spanking my ass as he took me against his bedroom wall the night our bond had been sealed filled my head. A shaky exhale escaped, and my thighs clenched against the sudden need that heated my core. Bennett's hands landed on my hips pulling me into him, my breasts rubbing against his hard chest. His fingers wrapped around my ponytail, his arousal growing to nudge against my stomach.

"Her powers have fully woken?" Jameson's question doused my untimely arousal as if he had dropped a cold bucket of water on me.

"Not all." Bennett reluctantly released me and stepped away not even trying to hide the bulge in his pants. A hot wave of embarrassment rushed across my cheeks as I turned to face the other men. *For god sakes, Lia, your grandfather is in the room.* Bennett was kryptonite to my willpower. That was my only excuse. Grayson gave me his boyish smile, clearly amused at my predicament. Bennett tucked me against his side, his hand settling possessively on my hip. Grayson flanked my other side, settling into his deceptively relaxed stance. The knowing smirk Jameson gave me told me he hadn't missed a thing.

"Now you," I tipped my head toward Jameson, avoiding

making eye contact with Giovanni. I wasn't going to be the only one showing off my mark.

Jameson's hands landed on his hips. "That wasn't part of the deal."

"My invite must have gotten lost in the mail for the original negotiations." My smile was all teeth. "I'm setting this new term of the deal. I showed you mine. Now you show me yours."

No one moved.

Giovanni's booming laugh split the silence. He spoke rapidly in Italian to Jameson. I was only able to catch part of what he said: "Hope is only a seed that cannot grow unless you nourish it with actions."

Jameson pulled his shirt off and threw it to the floor revealing a drool-worthy chest. I tried to keep my scan of his torso brief to avoid lighting the powder keg beside me. There wasn't a symbol on any of those tanned muscles. A condescending smile twisted his lips before he turned around. A gold sun symbol covered his back. The rays seemed to shimmer and dance under the harsh light of the room.

"But I thought ..." I looked at Bennett in confusion.

"Thought what?" Jameson gave me a smug smile over his shoulder. "That Kyrion Chaos—or should I call you *Bennett* since we're practically family—was the only one with a symbol on his back?"

He turned, not bothering to put the shirt back on and closed the distance between us so quickly he must have teleported. Bennett and Grayson pushed me behind them. Jameson gave them a bored look and peered down at me over their shoulders. "Your boyfriend may have been the only one born with the Archigós mark, but others have come into theirs over time. Like me."

Jameson stalked away as gracefully as a jaguar and every bit as deadly. He slid onto one of the loungers and gestured for us to join him. "Those with the Archigós mark are the most powerful descendants since the time the gods roamed the earth. Aside from the Chosen, of course. There have only been a few recorded in history," he informed me nonchalantly. Everyone settled onto a lounger except for Grayson, who stood diligently behind mine. This seemed to amuse our host as he stretched out on the lounger with his hands beneath his head. "Yet now they are appearing in nearly every House. Change is coming."

"Change is here," Giovanni stated firmly. "Show her."

"And he says I'm impatient," Jameson sighed dramatically. I was getting the feeling that drama was his middle name. "Fine. Lady and gentlemen, please don't be alarmed. This will only hurt a little."

Straps shot across my chest and legs securing me to the table. Grayson pulled a knife from his pants and tried to cut through them. The straps turned translucent and the knife slipped through as if they weren't there. The straps expanded across my whole body locking me down so I couldn't move; the only space was a bubble around my head. My heart flopped around in my chest as panic hit me, and my shout of alarm echoed against the barrier. My powers surged and fire enveloped my hands. Out of the corner of my eye, I saw fire shooting through the barrier that covered Bennett as he fought to get out.

It was no use. We were trapped.

Through the clear bindings I watched helplessly as Grayson tried to reach me. His frightened face was the last thing I saw before a glowing gold liquid poured into the bubble surrounding my head. My gasping breaths sounded loud in the enclosed space. Goose bumps pebbled my skin as the cold liquid filled in only around my head leaving the rest of me dry. I fought against taking a breath, but my oxygen-starved lungs finally gave out. Liquid poured into my mouth. Pain shot through my head straight down to my toes, and my mind was ripped from my body.

19

"Jillian!" The distorted sound of someone calling my name filtered through the lingering pain pounding through my head. I stood up, gasping for air, the room going in and out of focus around me. Images flickered past too fast to see clearly as I blinked, trying to figure out where I was. The pain faded away and a nondescript white room came into focus.

What had Jameson done to us? Where were Bennett and Grayson?

"Jilli-bean," a sing-song-y voice echoed around the small room. My mom was the only person who ever called me that. Shadows lengthened, and there she was—sitting on the edge of a bed nudging a lump beneath the covers as she called out playfully, "Come on sleepyhead. You're going to miss the sun."

The room shifted into my old bedroom at my parents' house. The purple walls of the room were lined with artwork and newspaper articles about my non-profit work. My twenty-two-year-old self peeked at my mom from her position on the bed, then pulled the covers back over her head. Mom laughed and pulled them back down. I looked so innocent in an oversized sleep shirt and tousled hair. Grumbling about it being too early, while barely managing to hold back a laugh as my mom played out her part of this familiar scene.

The shadows lengthened again, and there was my family sitting on the dock behind the house watching the sun rise. They lay on the ratty old blanket my mother refused to throw away, eating strawberries and talking about my future now that I was out of college. My father had always loved sunrises, which made sense now that I knew he was descended from Apollo. Their happy chatter surrounded me. This is the way I wanted to remember them. I didn't know why I was being shown these memories, but at the moment I was too grateful to care. If only I could stay here in this moment and never have to experience what happened next.

There had been years of my life when I denied that my parents, and this version of me, ever existed. But with Bennett's help I had learned to accept my past and face it. The pain and longing to have back the life that was destroyed on this day was still with me. It likely always would be, but I was strong enough to cherish this memory now and let it chase away some of the lingering darkness dwelling under my lonely highway.

The scene shifted again to our kitchen, showing my family goofing off as we packed for our trip out on the boat. My parents shared secretive smiles, brushing up against each other with a casual touch of the hand or hip bump. The love they had shared was a tangible force that made me ache to one day share that with Bennett. The younger version of me laughed at something they had said. For a moment, it was like looking at a complete stranger. She was so carefree and happy. If only I could alter the course of history and keep them from getting on that boat.

I had to try.

I grabbed for my mom's arm, but my hand slipped right through her. The same happened with my father. My shouts went unacknowledged. I tried to throw things or set something on fire, but my powers didn't seem to work here. Nothing worked. I stood in the middle of the kitchen floor, my chest heaving with desperation to change this. To save my parents and the girl I had once been. I knew what was coming but was helpless to prevent it. A hot ball of emotions churned inside me, and tears spilled down my cheeks. My eyes met my mom's, and she gave me a knowing smile.

Wait. Could she see me?

I rushed toward her, but she had already turned away. The scene shifted once more, and we were on the sailboat. The younger version of me was standing at the prow, loose hair whipping in the wind. Her head thrown back, soaking in the sun and the scents of the ocean. My parents stood at the ship's wheel watching the younger me with love and pride.

My father's dark brown eyes shifted to my mom and worry filled their depths. "How do you think she'll take the news?"

"Our Jilli-bean has always been strong and independent." My mom pushed her dark brown hair over her shoulder and placed her hand over my father's heart. "I just wish we could be there with her through everything that is coming. Henry, how can we leave her like this? The things I have seen in my visions ..."

"I know. I know, my star." My father pulled her to him and wiped the tears from her cheeks. "I would sacrifice everything to keep you both safe, but this is the way your visions have shown you it has to be. They have never been wrong. If she does not come into her powers and find the rest of the Chosen, all of the descendants will die."

"We don't know that for sure." My mom gripped his shirt, desperation turning her bright blue eyes a shade darker. "Maybe the stories your father told you were wrong. He is the protector of only one piece of the prophecy. You said yourself that the other pieces have been scattered amongst the Houses."

"No, we can't be certain." My dad cupped her cheek. "But you more than any other person have felt us weakening. Your guardians said the gods went to sleep to conserve their powers and wait for the time that the Order could be made whole again. That something went wrong, and they became trapped. We can't look to the gods to save us. We must save ourselves."

"You mean Jillian and her Chosen must save us." Mom rested her forehead against my father's chest. "I'm scared."

"I am too, Stella. I have thought a million times about going on the run again. But the fighting will never end unless the prophecy is fulfilled. And we can't outrun the bond curse." My father stoked her hair, his throat working rapidly to choke back his own tears. "Sometimes I wish that you had never seen me that night. That our bond-mate claiming had never happened so that you could live on forever. How could your father give our people this gift only to make it a curse that everyone who finds their true bond-mate will die?" Mom's head jerked up, but he quickly placed his finger to her lips. "No, I don't regret a moment of our bond or our life together. You are my guiding star and my heart. Even death will not keep us apart." He stroked her back soothingly and placed a gentle kiss on her lips. "We will fight until our last breath, but the end for us is her beginning. We will leave her every possible weapon we can. If the God of Chaos is merciful, we will watch over her from the stars."

My mother snorted. "He couldn't care less about mercy. We are only here for his entertainment."

"I doubt your guardians taught you that. You can't let what will happen to Lia steal your faith. The God of Chaos could have wiped us from the earth when his son fell and the Chaonian society collapsed." My father gripped her arms. His eyes roaming over her face as if memorizing every detail. "He has a plan for us. There is still hope. *She* is our hope."

Mom turned to look at me—the current incorporeal version of me—where I stood beside them. My heart skipped a beat as she spoke to me directly. How could she see me and no one else could? "Yes, she is our hope. And we will aid her in every way possible even if we can't be here with her."

The scene sped forward again, and our boat was under attack. This time I could see the powers that were being used to stir up the storm and the ocean. Lines of silver light speared into the sky calling forth the thunder and lightning. The storm raged overhead pouring buckets of water down on my family. Lightning struck the lake and thunder boomed, making the ship shake. My father was pulled overboard. My mother gripped the younger me, hugging her fiercely. Her lips were moving rapidly as she placed her hand upon the girl's back. My mom's eyes seemed to be boring straight into mine where I stood an invisible observer, helplessly watching it all unfold. Her lips moved still, but I couldn't hear a thing over the sounds of the storm.

Then a bright light enveloped the younger version of me and grew until everything was swallowed by the light.

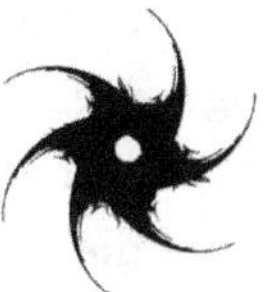

20

My eyes flew open, and I fought against the straps still holding me to the lounger back in the House of Light. The liquid sloshed wildly as I shook my head back and forth trying to get free. Bubbles rose from my mouth as I shouted. The now clear liquid that surrounded my head was warmer than before and missing the glow from earlier. High overhead the sky was visible through the honeycomb windows, the dark beginning to fade with the coming of the sun.

"*Lia!*" Bennett shouted through our connection.

"*I'm here!*" The pain from before was gone, but being trapped in this body condom was wreaking havoc on my nerves. "*I can't get out!*"

"*Jameson is freeing me now. Be calm, asteràki. I do not think they are trying to kill us, but be cautious.*"

"*Bennett, I saw things.*" My voice echoed the pain those memories brought back. "*I heard and saw things that never happened the day of the boat accident. How is that possible?*"

"*I think we all saw what you did,*" Bennett mused, the low growl of his voice stating more than words how pissed off he was right now. "*The only way that could be possible was if—*"

"If what? You can't leave me hanging like that. What were you going to say?"

"If there were someone else there that day, and we were seeing their memories, not yours." Bennett's voice was dark and menacing. *"If that is the case, then the House of Light could be involved in your parents' murders."*

I stopped struggling against the straps, my whole body turning cold as that thought hit me like an avalanche. My parents were *murdered*. My mother had known they were coming and that they would die. Yet they had gone out on that boat anyway. They had knowingly gone to their deaths to secure my future as Chosen. *No, they wouldn't do that to me! Please god, tell me they hadn't sacrificed themselves for me.* My vision wavered as my fingers clawed at the lounger. I couldn't breathe!

Giovanni's face appeared above me. "Be calm, Lia. You must stop fighting, or you will hurt yourself." His weathered hand pressed against the bubble surrounding my head as my mouth opened wide, struggling to find a breath. But there was no air, only the clear liquid burning through me with every swallow. "Jameson, she's having a panic attack! Get the blasted thing off her."

The restraining bubble disappeared. The liquid streamed from around my head and poured out of my mouth, as if someone was suctioning it from my lungs. Lights danced in my vision as it took the last of my breath with it. Gurgling sounds issued from my throat as the liquid lifted into the air in a reverse rain shower before disappearing. I curled over the side of the table coughing and gagging so hard my eyes felt as if they would pop out.

Grayson elbowed my grandfather out of the way, talking to me in a soothing voice as I shuddered through every wracking cough. My lungs filled with air as they tried to figure out how to function properly again, but it was little use as sobs replaced the coughing. My grandfather grasped my hand and placed a white handkerchief in it. Grayson continued to rub my back until there were no more tears left in me. I wiped my eyes and blew my nose. Then flopped onto my back feeling wrung out.

"I am sorry for this, but you had to know the truth of your parents' deaths." Giovanni smoothed away a lock of hair stuck to my forehead, his eyes full of pain and sadness as he looked down at me. "They loved you greatly, Lia. I am glad my only son found such happiness with you and your mother." Regrets carved new lines into his wrinkled face even as I watched, and my heart melted a bit toward him. Whatever had happened between them, he had loved his son.

Garbled words poured from my lips, but Grayson got the gist and helped me to sit up. The sounds of a fight reached me. Bennett and Jameson danced around each other trading punches. Both were bleeding from various cuts. Bennett launched into a rapid-fire series of kicks that got past Jameson's guard and dropped him to his back. Jameson quickly rolled to his feet and laughed as he tackled my furious bond-mate. We had become allies with a madman. I turned my head away, not having the energy to deal with them.

I pushed my surprisingly dry hair away from my face and stopped short at the sight of my hands. My throat burned still, and my words came out barely above a whisper when I said, "W-why am I g-gl-lowing?"

"The memory serum," Giovanni replied. "It is liquid sunlight and a mixture of other things our scientists have come up with. The light is a part of who you are and recognizes you as it would any of Apollo's children."

My powers finished healing my throat, and I jumped

from the lounger, putting some distance between myself and any other furniture in this room. Who knew what other surprises they hid? Grayson angled himself into a position slightly between me and my grandfather. Giovanni nodded to the young man, as if he respected Grayson's dedication to my protection. A flicker of movement caught my attention, and I looked up at the Jumbotron. Everything I had seen under the influence of the serum was playing there in a continuous loop.

I quickly averted my eyes. As I did so, the control panel we had passed on the way into this room caught my attention. *They had known exactly what they were doing leading us in here.* Anger lit up the powers at my center. What kind of people subjected their allies to a forced memory dump without our consent? Who the fuck did they think they were?

"Listen here Zen-master-lightbulb, I've already got a Yoda-wannabe stuck to me like I sat in gum." I gestured at Grayson, who grinned at me unrepentantly. "Can you give me the House of Light Training Manual for Dummies version of what the hell just happened? Cuz I'm two seconds from lighting up like a bonfire, and this looks like a no-smoking area."

When Giovanni gave me a puzzled look, Grayson translated. "My lady's patience for diplomacy has ended and further provocation of her temper will result in fire. Most likely thrown at your expensive equipment. She does not appreciate being taken by surprise and wishes to understand what was done to her." Grayson motioned to the Jumbotron. "How is this possible? Please explain in simple terms."

"Ah yes, simple is best." The twinkle in Giovanni's eyes said he was amused by us, but I didn't give a shit. I would torch their mind-melding equipment in a heartbeat if they made one more wrong move. Only a few months ago I would have been embarrassed about threatening someone. Now threaten or maim first was becoming a way of life. If only people would take me seriously. My threats were not cute, dammit!

Giovanni cleared his throat as I continued to glare at him and said, "The memories you saw were from a man we captured several months ago. He was sent to steal the piece of the prophecy that I guard." Giovanni pushed aside the collar of his robes to reveal a pale pink line that looked like a scar from a knife wound. "I am not so easy to kill. What Jameson said earlier about his family being against the killing of the Paldimori was mostly true."

My grandfather looked at the floor and shook his head in shame. "His uncle, however, was an exception. The man was cruel and vain. The Olympian Omàda played to those weaknesses, and he was their puppet. Through him, they gained access to our technology, using it against us to brainwash our children into doing their killing and delving into the minds of those they captured to find the locations of the Paldimori Houses." Giovanni's sorrow was a hard thing to witness. "Jameson's father challenged his brother and killed him to become our Kyrion. That was eight years ago. Jameson took over when his father was killed three years ago and began actively working against the Omàda. We have been tracking down the serum to reclaim it from them and subtly stalling their efforts where we can."

Could I trust what I saw, or was this another trick? There were so many questions. Then something Giovanni said triggered a memory. My hands shook as Titan's voice echoed through my head again. *"Find the twin Houses of the Olympian Omàda."* It couldn't be this easy, could it?

"You know who the Olympian Omàda is?" I asked, holding my breath in anticipation of his answer.

Giovanni nodded slowly, watching me with concern. "Did your parents not teach you of your people? Of our history, child?"

"Until three months ago I had no idea your world existed," I confessed. Giovanni's shock may have been the only forthright thing about this meeting. "My parents gave up their names, their families, everything to give me a life free from your fighting. From the blind hatred between the Houses. They wanted a better life for me." Tears clogged my voice as the images I saw when they put me in their shrink-wrap mind-probe thing played through my head again. They were real. I knew they were. "When the fight came to our door anyway, they sacrificed their own lives to give me a better chance at surviving all of you. Don't you dare blame them for any of this."

Giovanni's lined face had grown haggard. "I do not blame them, child." His hand trembled when he reached out to me. I hesitated for a moment looking for signs of deceit. Betrayal had become as common as the cold around me, and it was catching. Yet they could have killed us all while Bennett and I were under the influence of the serum. My hand was engulfed in his before I could overthink it. He smiled and patted my hand. "My son made the hard choices that I was too afraid to make. I gave up the woman who could have been my bond-mate for my duties. She passed away several years ago, and now all I am left with are regrets. You and your Bennett share a very strong bond, even I could feel it. I am very proud of my son and of you."

"Thank you," I said, wiping the tears from my eyes. Grayson moved closer, pressing his shoulder against mine to offer me comfort.

Giovanni's eyes were suspiciously bright when he patted my hand one last time and cleared his throat. "Well, then, we have much to cover. Your history lessons begin now." He tucked his hands into his robes. His brow furrow as he focused on some distant past.

"The Houses were not always enemies. In the beginning there was only the Primordial Gods—Chaos, Gaia, Eros, Erebus, Tartarus, and Nyx—the children of the God of Chaos. Then came the human children of God."

Giovanni sighed. "Curiosity is a weakness for god or man. The Primordial Gods began to breed with the humans and created halflings—demigods. The first few children born to the gods were bound in servitude to Chaos, and he called these twelve Titans. And there began the sowing of his own demise." Giovanni made a clicking sound with his tongue in reproach. "We will discuss that in more detail at a later time.

"Now, the first Houses were founded by the six Primordial Gods to protect their halfling offspring. Ruled over by Chaos, they called their people Chaonians and created a sanctuary on the island of Atlantaionia. The Titans were the strongest of all the halflings and hated the weaker siblings who came after them. They asked to be free to live on their own on Mount Olympus and the request was granted. There they renamed themselves the Olympians." Giovanni scowled and removed his hands from his pockets to shake a fist at the sky. "And what did they do? Betrayed their parents, intending to kill the weak and take over. But Chaos stood against them, wielding the sword they called the Achlys—the god-killer. He drained the power from the land to—"

"Time-out. There were twelve of them? On Mount Olympus? You're talking about the Olympian gods, aren't you?" I asked in astonishment. Giovanni nodded. My gaze wandered back over the twelve loungers in this room. Shit on a shingle, the Olympian Omàda were the Olympian gods, and now their descendants. Finally, I had a name for the enemies of the Paldimori, and I was standing in their midst. "I read somewhere that the Chaonian War was started when the firstborns attacked the gods. That was them. The Olympian gods turned on their parents—the Primordials." I shot my grandfather an accusing look. "The House of Light is part of the Olympian Omàda!"

"We were once," Giovanni said sadly. "Jameson's father made a deal with Kyrion Zeus from the House of Storms, leader of the Omàda. He had finally found proof—"

A fireball shot through the ceiling above. We all ducked for cover as glass and wood fell down around us. Grayson crowded me protectively beneath him. Across the room Jameson disappeared. Bennett stood still as a statue, his eyes the only thing moving as he searched out his target. Blood trickled from his nose and mouth. His shirt was missing half of its buttons and holes were burned into the fabric. His jeans were ripped, and one thigh was soaked in blood. Suddenly his hand shot toward a spot to his right. Jameson reappeared dangling from the hand Bennett had wrapped around his neck.

Stupid testosterone-filled men. The only way they knew to solve their differences was through their fists. My powers lit up, and I stroked my hand over the glowing ball. *That's right girl, let's show them how a woman ends an argument.* The light filled me as I fed it everything I was feeling: heartache at finding out that my parents had given their lives for me; anger at Giovanni and Jameson's trick; uncertainty about my future and where we went from here; and the nagging worry that time was running out for all of us.

I teleported across the room, and for once I landed on my feet exactly where I wanted to be. My palms smacked against a muscled chest on either side of me. "Enough!" I shouted. "I've had a really rotten day. I need pj's. Then food and a bed. Preferably a boatload of chocolate somewhere in the middle of all that. If one of you douche nozzles doesn't get me those things soon, I'm going to be a hangry little Chosen that goes nuclear on both your asses."

Bennett ripped off a hanging piece off his shirt to wipe away the blood on his face. I was pretty sure he was covering up a smile, but he had the sense not to let me see it. Jameson wasn't as smart. He laughed. That fucknugget actually *laughed* at me. My fist landed on his jaw, backed by my eager powers. His head snapped back, and he fell to the floor with a thud—out cold. Click must have taken this as his sign because he left his holster on my leg to draw a bag full of cocks on Jameson's cheek. My laughter was a bit on the crazy side. Yeah, I was going to hell for being the worst parent ever, but Click was right—the guy really was a dickbag.

Grayson and Giovanni walked over to look down at the unconscious Kyrion. They eyed me warily and with surprise.

"Why does no one take me seriously when I threaten them?" I huffed. "When the drama queen wakes up, tell him I said next time to start off with chocolate and conversation. I've had too many people attacking me. Surprises make me twitchy."

21

Why we were up at the butt-crack of dawn, I had no idea. Especially when we had only teleported back from Sicily a few hours ago. There had been so much to discuss after our trip, but we had all been too bone-weary to tackle it right away and had agreed to talk about it later on today. Grayson knocked on my bedroom door when the sun was still only a faint notion on the horizon, saying, through the door, that my presence was requested.

I lay in bed staring at the ceiling as tears slipped from the corners of my eyes. Sleep hadn't come easy since every time I closed my eyes my mind kept conjuring up images of my parents on the deck of our ship clasping hands and saying they were doing this for me before they jumped to their deaths. Bennett had tried to comfort me as we made our way back down the elevator in the House of Light last night, but I was so angry with him. He had not only known about my grandfather but had left me out of decisions that had to do with *my* life. And I couldn't help but wonder if he had known my parents had been murdered. I wanted to hunt Bennett down and tie him to a chair until he gave up all of his secrets.

A knock sounded at the door again, and Lydia stepped inside. "My lady, the weapons-master has asked that you and Kyrion Bennett come to his shop." She shifted uncomfortably as I continued to stare at the ceiling not bothering to hide my wet cheeks. She'd likely never seen a Kyrion—or one in training, anyway—cry before.

"*Go now,*" the ghostly voice of Calidora whispered near my ear, her cold presence jarring me from my cocoon of grief. "*Time is short, Chosen.*"

My gaze shifted to her picture above my bed and a torrent of emotions swamped me. I jumped to my feet and ripped the painting from the wall.

"My lady!" Lydia shrieked in horror.

"Leave me alone," I shouted stumbling backward over the bed with the heavy painting in my hands as Lydia cowered against the mirror, calling for help. All of my insecurities and doubts became tangled with the pit of guilt and grief eating away at me. "Do you hear me, Calidora? Just leave me alone. I'm not you or Selene. I'm a human-raised substitute that will never be your equal." I sobbed as the weight of everything threatened to break me into little pieces. "My parents—"

I tripped over the blankets with a cry and fell face down on the bed. The painting slipped from my hands hitting the floor with a loud crack as the frame broke. My stomach sank as I saw who stood inside my doorway. Selene and Guide Athan observed me resolutely as if they had known all along that I was unfit for this world. Grayson gave me a sad look filled with sympathy and worry. But it was the disbelief and pain on Bennett's face that made me want to crawl into a hole.

"Bennett," I whispered, reaching out for him.

He turned away and left the room without a word.

Selene stepped forward to take charge, but I pulled the blanket to my chest and said quietly, "I want you all to leave."

"Lia, you have lessons—"

"No, Selene," I cut her off. "I'll go to *Mark's* as requested but there will be no lessons today. No training. No dresses." I made eye contact with each one of them. "I tried to be what you wanted but I can only be me. Starting now."

Grayson ushered the morose crowd out of my room and bent to pick up the painting before I stopped him. "Leave it. I'll meet you downstairs."

I got dressed and sat on the floor staring at the painting. "I'm sorry, Calidora." *Gods what a mess I had made of this bond-mate-Kyrion thing.* "Now you know. I'm not as brave or tough as I pretend. Everything that has happened since I touched that stupid invite for the Games has been piling on me as if the gods want to test how much I can take. Finding out my parents were murdered last night—that they gave up their lives for mine—was the last straw." My head dropped into my hands. "I was broken before your son found me, and I'm even more broken now. I don't know what I have to offer to Bennett or your people, but I'm still going to try. I just can't do it living in your shadow anymore."

I felt the weight of every one of those rocks that had been piling on me as I tried to piece myself back together and move on from this morning's disaster. A cold hand smoothed down my back and for the first time Calidora called me by name. *"Lia, child, you are not broken. The gods challenge all who are capable of greatness. It is a testament to your strength that you keep trying."* That cold hand gripped my shoulder. *"You are the warrior-queen my son and our people need. You walk in no one's shadow, my daughter."*

A sob caught in my throat. "I wish I could have met you when you were alive."

"As do I, daughter, but I am here with you now as are so many others that believe in you." Calidora's voice began to fade. *"Go do what you must, but beware, daughter, the enemy is closer than you think, and a great darkness draws nearer every day."*

I could see now why Calidora was so beloved. I stood and picked up the painting, wincing at the damaged gold frame. At least the painting itself seemed mostly unharmed. A small black velvet draw-string bag fell from a hollowed-out part of the frame when I lifted it.

"Hurry, my lady, the Kyrion is preparing to leave," Grayson informed me telepathically.

I shoved the bag into my jeans pocket and hurried downstairs where Bennett was waiting. Our not-so-merry band exited the mansion and walked along the silent streets toward the center of the city. Bennett walked far ahead and hadn't looked at me once since I had joined the group. My eyes burned, and my body felt heavy with fatigue from lack of sleep and the emotional upheaval. Goose bumps pebbled my arms as a chill breeze cut through the morning air.

The smell of burning coals and the sound of a heavy hammer hitting metal greeted us as we entered Mark's shop. The guides fanned out around the room as Bennett and I walked to the open doorway behind the counter and into a room that looked like an old blacksmith's forge. Weapons in different stages of completion hung from the ceiling off to the left. A low stone bed attached to a hearth took up most of the right side of the room. Mark paused with his massive hammer mid-swing when he noticed us at the door. The glowing hot piece of metal that he had been about to strike on the anvil lifted into the air and drove itself into the bed of coals at the hearth. His tools rearranged themselves into their respective places hanging on the wall or in barrels sitting around the floor. Mark took off his heavy gloves and apron, and they too flew through the air to find their home.

The big man pulled a rag from his pocket to wipe his hands and sweat-covered face. "My lord. My lady," he greeted us in his raspy voice and bowed deeply.

"How many times do I have to tell you not to bow to me?" Bennett admonished.

"Maybe when you're no longer Kyrion, I'll listen." Mark flashed his crooked smile. "When will you learn to respect your elders?"

"You may be older but that does not mean wiser," Bennett countered with a chuckle. "You still let Devon talk you into playing cards with him even though you know he cheats."

It was hard to image Devon—the gruff and always serious leader of the guides—cheating at anything. What little I had gotten to know about him during the first competition said he was all about rules and keeping people in line. He wasn't a big fan of mine and had even told me once that I talked too much. I could have told him that after years of isolating myself and locking everything away under the thick pavement of my lonely highway that I was making up for lost time, but for some reason I liked nettling the man.

"Little brother hasn't gotten a trick past me since he snuck off with one of Daddy's cigars when he was eleven and tried to blame me. Besides, I appreciate the free beer," Mark chuckled hoarsely. "But you didn't come here to talk about my brother's poor poker face." He walked to the back of the room and pulled something wrapped in cloth from the shelf. Then handed the object to Bennett. "I have finished what you asked for."

Mark turned to me and pulled a necklace from his pants pocket. Under the lights of the room the black chain shimmered with various colors similar to the ring on my finger. "And for you, my lady."

"Thank you, Mark, but you didn't have to do this. You already gave us gifts."

"This is no ordinary necklace," Mark informed me. "May I, my lady?"

I turned to allow him to place the chain around my neck. The cool touch of the metal quickly turned to a comforting warmth as it settled into place. "It will react to your will and form a tunic of armor. Think of a shield wrapping around you and push that thought into the necklace."

I did as he instructed. A silky blanket of warmth climbed up my neck, and I watched in amazement as black liquid poured down my arms, and finally down my chest all the way to my hips. The liquid hardened into interlocking swirls of flames, like fancy chainmail but lightweight and very flexible. My unique symbol with all its various colors sat like the crowning jewel between my breasts. "Mark, you're a genius!"

Mark walked me through releasing the armor and told me the more I practiced the quicker the transition would become. Bennett nodded approvingly. Then glanced at the cloth-covered package in his hands and back to me. I got the impression he was weighing whether or not he should share this with me. After damaging his mother's painting this morning, I doubted he wanted to share anything with me right now. *"Please, Bennett, let me explain."*

"I know that you were hurt that I had not told you about your grandfather or the negotiations that had taken place. I am sorry for that and the pain you must be feeling after all we saw

last night." Bennett clutched the cloth-wrapped package with white knuckles. "*Were those sins so great that you would strike back at me by trying to destroy my mother's painting?*"

"*No! I would never do something so cruel.*" I struggled to find the words to explain. Would he believe me if I told him about his mother's ghost? Would I want to know my parents were still lingering but had never reached out to me in all these years? "*Your mother was a good woman who loved you very much. I-I was wild with grief over my parents' murders and let my own insecurities drive me to lash out. I'm so sorry, Bennett.*"

Bennett bowed his head for a moment and when he looked up, I breathed a sigh of relief. He gave me a tentative smile and said, "*I know how grief can drive a person to do things that they regret.*"

A dark shadow of self-loathing seemed to flicker across his face. It was gone so quickly I wondered if it hadn't been a trick of the lighting. A grim disquiet gnawed at me. Was there still more that he was hiding?

"*My mother is not a yardstick that you must measure yourself against,*" Bennett said carefully. "*I realize now that it is my own fault that you may have gotten that impression. I pushed Selene upon you and let her take full control of your introduction to becoming a Kyrion. Yes, there is much for you to learn, but I never wanted you to be anyone except yourself.*"

I almost sank to the floor under the release of pressure. "*Thank you, Bennett.*" I placed my hand over his where it rested on top of the cloth package. "*It seems we need to work on being more open and communicating with each other, husband.*"

"*Indeed, wife,*" Bennett turned his hand over to squeeze mine and raised it to his lips. "*I look forward to practicing all manner of husbandly duties with you.*"

Heat filled my cheeks as I glanced at Mark who gave me a warm smile, and I hurriedly excused myself so the men could talk business. Grayson pushed away from the wall and followed me. I crossed to the right side of the room and stepped into the first alcove I came to. As if he sensed my need for privacy, Grayson stationed himself at the opening with his back toward me, blocking me from view. A collection of spears lined the walls in various shapes, sizes, and colors. I pressed the heels of my hands hard against my eyes. This day had already been an emotional rollercoaster and the sun was barely up.

A low thrumming caught my attention. There was that pull again, like I had experienced at the hot springs, as if I were being drawn toward something. I began to walk, allowing the thrumming rhythm to lead me. Grayson took up position in the center of the shop so that he could watch me no matter where I went. The thrumming increased in tempo as I passed the alcove of swords. I backtracked and tried walking past again. Whatever was calling to me was definitely in this area. I stepped into the alcove, scanning the sword-covered walls from floor to ceiling. Every type of blade imaginable—and maybe a few never seen outside of this city—were displayed. They ranged from swords as tall as me to tiny knives no bigger than my thumb. A medium-sized sword with a black blade caught my eye. My fingers traced over the smooth surface, and it felt as if the metal heated beneath my touch. The thrumming noise hit a crescendo, then fell silent.

"Are you going to kill our Kyrion?" a small voice asked, making me jump and cut my finger on the sword.

I sucked in a sharp breath at the pain, and a trickle of blood slid across the black sword. It absorbed into the metal, and faint blue swirls lit up the blade. A vision filled my mind of Titan wielding the weapon as he battled against several other male and female figures. The sword glowed a bright blue as the god hacked through a red ball of power, making it disappear. I blinked, wondering if I had really seen any of that. Lack of sleep must have been catching up with me.

I shook my head, dismissing the images, and searched the space for my unexpected visitor. "Who's there?"

"The people in town say you're going to kill Kyrion Bennett, and then the bad people will come." A young girl around nine or ten with light brown skin and pigtails, peeked her head over the ledge above the alcove doorway. "You don't look evil. Not like Mrs. Lasterman. She has weird eyes and lipstick on her teeth. She gave us homework on the first day of school."

"Uh, I don't think I'm evil. Why would people say I'm going to kill the Kyrion?" Good to know I didn't look like an evil teacher, but why the hell would people think I was going to kill my husband? "Ben—uh, Kyrion Bennett is very important to me. I would never hurt him."

"You might be soul bonded." Her dark eyes assessed me curiously. "Then the Kyrion can die. I don't ever want to have a bond-mate. Daddy could have died when Mommy did if they had completed the bond. I wouldn't have a mommy or a daddy now. Are you going to have babies?"

What the ever-loving hell? Our bonding meant that Bennett would *die*? My father's voice from the memories I had seen in Sicily filled my head: *"How could your father give our people this gift only to make it a curse that everyone who finds their true bond-mate will die?" I had been so distraught at seeing my parents die again and learning that they had been murdered that I had forgotten that part of the memories.*

No, no, no! I can't be responsible for someone else giving up their life for me.

"What does it—" I started to ask the girl questions, but Mark, Bennett, and Grayson joined us before I got the chance.

"Kayla Ann, come down here and stop harassing our future Kyrion." Mark's exasperated voice cut me off. The girl jumped from the ledge, turning a somersault in the air, and landed on her feet. My mouth dropped open in astonishment at her skill. She gave me a wide grin and then sprinted out the door.

"I'm sorry, my lady," Mark said sheepishly. It was disconcerting to see a man twice my size wringing his hands nervously. "My daughter has run a bit wild since my wife died last year."

"Mark, it's ok." I forced another smile. At this point I would have my sociable smile down pat for future Kyrion duties. "And I'm sorry for your loss."

"Thank you, my lady," he replied. My brain was turning over what the girl had said and making connections that had me fighting my need to grab Bennett and stake him out in the desert until he spilled every thought in his head. Mark gestured toward my hand. "My daughter found this sword near the hot springs. It seems the landslide uncovered it. I finished cleaning it just this morning. Did you want to try the sword, my lady?"

The sword with the black blade was still in my hand, posed for a strike, as if I knew what I was doing. I hadn't even realized that I'd picked it up. Calidora had called me a warrior-queen, maybe this was part of what she meant. It fit my hand well enough, but somehow, I got the impression that it was destined for someone else. "I'll take the sword," I declared as my grip tightened around the hilt.

Click wiggled from the holster on my leg, circling around the sword and making clicking noises as if he approved. Mark went to find whatever accessories I would need for my new weapon. There must have been some sign of the desperate denial mounting inside me over what Kayla Ann had said because Bennett reached for our connection. His voice buzzed in the background of my mind asking what was wrong but there was too much to say.

My gaze met Bennett's. *"We need to talk."*

We teleported back to the foyer of Bennett's house. The guides dispersed, and Grayson went off to harass Selene. Bennett and I were left alone. We stared at each other, neither of us willing to be the first to speak. Then Bennett motioned for me to walk with him. He led me to the conference room where the monitors showed each of the six guard towers surrounding the base of the mountain. I noticed that there were a lot of Talosi gathered at each tower before Bennett turned off the screens.

I laid my new sword in its leather scabbard on the table and walked over to the fireplace. Concentrating on the logs, I coaxed my powers to flow out through my fingertips. The logs caught fire but, for once, it was a controlled flame, and nothing blew up. Finally, I was starting to get the hang of this.

"Well done, asteràki," Bennett said from close behind me. "You are learning quickly now that you have accepted that your powers and your emotions are a part of you."

I didn't respond. My mind was swirling with the realization that Bennett would die because of me. The deaths already on my hands flashed through my mind: the man from the streets, James, Grace, and my parents. The last unbroken section of pavement on my lonely highway rumbled, threatening to crack wide open and release my darkest nightmares.

Bennett's fingers brushed along my back, but I refused to turn around, needing a moment to compose myself.

The whispers I had overheard at the Bonding Ceremony about losing him and the look on Guide Athan's face made sense now. Everyone but me had known that bonding was a death sentence. I was surprised that they hadn't burned me at the stake to prevent us from claiming each other. I understood the vows now—mind, body, and soul. Bennett and I were irrevocably joined in life, as we would be in death.

"Don't," I said as Bennett's hands ran over my back in soothing strokes. I shrugged him off and turned around.

"Lia, what is it?" Bennett's brows knit in worry as he stepped closer.

"I want the truth. Not telepathically or rooting through your emotional bank vault to find out for myself. I want an honest conversation like we're a normal couple," I demanded with a hard edge to my voice that halted him in his tracks. "Got it?"

Bennett's eyes narrowed clearly hating my ordering him around, but he nodded in agreement.

"The day of our Bonding Ceremony, there were murmurs in the crowd about losing you." Bennett held completely still watching me behind the mask of the Kyrion. "Under the memory serum last night, my parents talked about a bond curse. And just now Mark's daughter told me that you could die because we would become bond-mates. Is that true? Will you die if I do?"

"Yes," he stated gruffly.

"For god's sake, Bennett," I choked out. "Why didn't you tell me?"

"Because you did not need to know."

"You don't get to decide that!" I shouted, anger and hurt boiled up inside of me looking for an outlet. "Fucking hell, Bennett, I thought we were past this. Didn't we just talk about being open and communicating with each other. Lies and omissions are what ripped us apart before. Yet, you still didn't say a word about our bond stripping away your immortality."

"I am not immortal. Only the gods and the first couple of children born to them were immortal," he said. An exasperated *"Arrr"* left me at Mr. Know-it-all correcting me even during an argument. Bennett gripped my hand in his and formed twin flames on my palm. "The Kyrion are the closest thing our people know to immortals because the strength of our power sustains our lives. The stronger the powers, the longer we live, and the harder we are to kill." The two flames joined as one and shrank in size. "When two people who are blessed by the gods to find their other half go through the bond-mate vows, it creates a soul deep connection; it combines our powers to form one source to sustain two lives. This is why finding a bond-mate is both a blessing and a curse. The length of our lives is shortened, and if one dies so does the other. Most of our people only go through the ceremony and never complete the vows to form the Desmòs. They are never willing to risk either shortening their lives or finding out their chosen bond-mate is not who the gods intended for them."

I watched the flame flicker and die out. "How can that be? I died when I got shot by that arrow, but you were fine."

"Your healing powers were working to keep you alive

and tied to this world." Bennett crowded into me, pushing my chin up to force me to meet his gaze. "We are one, Lia, in every possible way. Our lives are intertwined now, and I would change nothing. There is no world where I would choose to live if you died, and now that is impossible."

I jerked out of his grasp. "Why couldn't you have told me all of that before? You promised me that we were in this together, but you're still the one calling all the shots. We're either partners or we're nothing." Bennett flinched as I let my disappointment and heartbreak crash through the door to our connection before slamming it closed once more. "How can I trust you when you keep everything from me?"

"Trust?" Bennett scoffed, gripping my arms tightly. His eyes blazed with anger, and the fireplace behind me flared in reaction. "You have never fully trusted me. Yes, I made many mistakes when we first met. I have apologized and tried to be the 'boyfriend' you wanted." His sneer said more than words ever could how much he had hated that title. "You are the one who keeps me at arm's length, rarely opening your end of our connection. I have given you my love. Shared my life force with you. You will soon be co-ruler of my House. I have left my side of our connection open and invited you in to see all of me. Is that not enough?"

"I don't want to have to use our connection to search out the truths you bury!" I cried, shoving at his chest and not moving him an inch. "I don't want to learn who you are by digging through your memories and emotions. All I've ever wanted was honesty, and for you to show me who you are through actions and words." I teleported out of his hold and wrapped my arms around my body. I felt as if every word he said was a sharp claw digging into me, ripping and shred-ding. He didn't understand that he had the power to shatter me. That he could bury me back under the lonely highway that I had only just resurrected myself from. I feared if I ever went back to that, I might never surface again. "You're right," I said, "I haven't opened myself fully to you. You hurt me once, and I've kept a distance between us to lessen the blow when you hurt me again. Looks like I was right to protect myself."

Bennett's fist slammed down onto the conference table splitting it in half. "How could I possibly earn your trust when you continue to run from me? Even now you are pushing me away and putting distance between us." Bennett gestured toward the broken table between us.

Guides and Talosi burst into the room with their swords drawn. They took in the busted table and the face-off going on across it. No one moved. Then Guide Athan stepped forward motioning for everyone to lower their weapons. The swords were put away, but we were all still on edge.

Guide Athan bowed to Bennett and said, "Kyrion, it is time. The competition will begin any moment."

Bennett's jaw ticked madly as he coldly demanded, "See my bond-mate to her room and notify Selene that I wish to see her immediately. I teleport to Sotirìa in ten minutes."

"Now who's running," I snapped.

"I have duties to attend to," Bennett replied, that cold mask of the Kyrion back in place. He picked up my sword and held it out to me. "We will talk when I return."

I grabbed the sword, but he held on to it, watching me with an assessing look that said he expected me to run away as soon as he left. The mistrust cut at my already battered heart. My days of running were over, and I would prove it to him. "I'll be here," I stated with grim determination.

Selene teleported into the room and cleared her throat.

Bennett released the sword and walked away with Selene in tow. Anger, hurt, and frustration ignited a deadly cocktail inside me as I watched them leave. The Talosi assigned to me remained. They shifted uneasily as my clenched fists caught fire and my breath sawed in and out. My control slipped farther from my grip with each passing moment, undoing all of the progress I had made. I gathered the powers bursting at my center and teleported.

Water closed in over my head dousing the flames as I sank into the pool in Bennett's basement. I poured every thought and emotion into the scream that ripped from my mouth and sent a tidal wave of water sloshing over the side of the pool. The release of energy drained my strength, and I struggled to reach the surface. I broke through with a gasp and rolled onto my back to float. I closed my eyes letting the tension leach from my body and the quiet sooth my jagged emotions.

I don't know how long I had been floating when a whirring noise caught my attention. I looked around, treading water, but didn't see anyone. Suddenly, I was yanked underwater. My nose burned, and my chest ached as I sank toward the bottom. I tried to swim for the surface but a wave of water slammed into my chest. My breath exploded out in a spray of bubbles as I sank even further and hit the bottom of the pool, where a strong pressure held me, and I realized someone had opened the drain. The water moved unnaturally above me and for a moment I could almost make out the shape of a body. My hair whipped around me in the water as the suction from the drain seemed to get increasingly stronger. I realized what was going to happen seconds before my long locks were pulled into the drain and my head smashed against the floor of the pool.

Lights burst behind my eyes as I struggled not to take a

breath. My head throbbed from the impact and the pain of my hair being ripped from my scalp a strand at a time. I grabbed my hair with both hands and twisted onto my stomach trying to pull free. No matter how hard I tugged I couldn't get loose. I tried to teleport, but I had drained too much energy during my outburst. I sent out a mental call to Grayson and whoever else could hear me.

My struggles became weaker as my breath grew scarce and blackness loomed at the edges of my vision. My fingers spasmed and a hard object filled my right hand.

My sword!

I grasped the hilt with the last of my strength and swung, slicing through my hair. I was free of the drain but there was no more air left. Water rushed in to fill my mouth and lungs. Darkness edged closer as if I were looking down a long tunnel. Suddenly arms wrapped around me, pulling me toward the surface. Grayson shouted something but it sounded far away. He rolled me onto the concrete floor beside the pool and started CPR. My head lulled to the side as he started compressions, and I saw a ghostly Calidora holding hands with my parents as they watched on in agony.

My stomach lurched and I turned over onto my side, heaving up water and what little food I'd eaten. Grayson's warm palm on my shoulder felt like an anchor in the storm as sound and sensation rushed back to me. When my breathing had settled back to normal, Grayson wrapped his arms around me and teleported us to my bedroom. I went to the bathroom to change into dry clothes provided by the magic trunk and stood staring at the uneven sections of my hair. My hair had been one of my favorite features about myself and now that had been taken from me too. I padded back into the bedroom and sat down on the edge of the bed feeling numb.

"Please rest, my lady," Grayson pleaded in a shaky voice, his face pale and dotted with sweat. "Twice now I have come too close to losing you. God of Chaos be merciful and let there not be a third time."

23

———

The sensation of a tug along my back woke me with a start. My body ached after the near drowning at the pool. My heart ached for an entirely different reason as I remembered the things Bennett and I had said to each other. The midday sun shone through the tall windows of my bedroom, indicating I had been asleep for several hours. My stiff muscles protested every move as I sat up and scooted to the edge of the bed.

The tugging along my back became more insistent. The shadows around the room lengthened as if they were reaching for me. Whispers filled the air sounding like rushing water. Fire erupted along my spine bowing my back and a scream burst from my throat. I vaguely heard Grayson shouting my name. Then my body shattered into a million pieces. Moments later, I materialized under a star-filled sky, bent over, and breathing heavily through the nausea.

Whoever had teleported me here had done it at super-speed. Finally, I straightened, taking a shaky breath. The bright yellow galaxy I had seen when Dia was claimed by Gaia filled the night sky above me.

Fuck no, not again!

Where this weirdo went, pain was sure to follow.

"Creation." That emotionless voice rang through my head like a gong. *"You are not as you were but not yet what you will be."*

"That's not cryptic or anything," I shouted to the heavens in irritation. "The first time we met you wore my body, and then tossed it off like a cheap prom dress. Now you've sucked me up like confetti into a giant vacuum to deposit me wherever the hell this is. Who are you, and what do you want from me?"

Silence was the only response.

"You really need to work on your communication skills." These damn gods were a pain in the ass. The least they could do was pick up a phone if they needed to talk instead of invading my body or yanking me all over the place. "Hey, are you listening? If you're going to keep dropping into my life, the least you could do is bring chocolate.

"If that's you, Titan, I know what you're going to say," I sighed, playing down the fear that was keeping my stomach roiling. Nothing good happened when this guy talked to me, and I already felt raw from everything that had happened these last few days. I needed time to adjust to my new reality, but the gods didn't seem to believe in downtime. "Let me guess. It's something like: 'Find the twin Houses, blah, blah, blah.' Not that you care, but it's been a helluva week. How 'bout we skip the fortune cookie tidbits tonight? I could use a vacation."

A tendril of power slammed into my back shattering all thought and reason. It blasted through my body scorching every inch of me from the inside out. At my center, green light spilled from my glowing ball of power. Vines shot from my palms and curled up my arms. The vines twined themselves over my chest and down my legs digging into the ground to anchor me in place. What was happening to me? My teeth chattered as an icy rain fell, soaking me in seconds. The night filled with the distant sounds of wolves howling.

"*Become!*" the cold voice from the heavens demanded.

The starlight overhead brightened until my eyes stung. A male form materialized from the fabric of the night sky— his body a black canvas covered with stars. His eyes glowing white orbs that melted into a familiar swirling kaleidoscope of color. My voice was nothing more than a whispered groan as I acknowledged him. "Titan."

"Blood of my beloved, we meet again," Titan greeted me, his husky accented voice filling the space as if coming from every direction. Shivers wracked my body as I struggled to release myself from the vines. "Save your strength, little Chosen, I see the questions you would ask. I am here because a connection formed when you woke me from my slumber, and I felt your new powers born." He walked closer watching me like I was a curious bug. "I know you have already found one of the twin Houses, even if you have not yet realized this. My connection to this world is growing, and I am learning it anew."

His body changed into a man with long black hair that swept the ground and a naked heavily muscled body. Here we go again with the nakedness. I shifted my gaze back to the starlit sky above, making a mental note that the creeper from earlier had disappeared as soon as Titan materialized. "Yet there are some things veiled from me. The imprint of my father's presence still lingers here. Tell me, what was it the God of Chaos said to you?"

"That's the creeper who keeps showing up like a bad penny? I thought the cryptic asshole in my head a few minutes ago was you." The cold rain slid down my face, and the vines tightened around me. All I had left at this moment was attitude and anger. I was done being the dancing fool they trotted out to perform for them when and how they wanted. "I'm gonna need an asshole-sorting process so I can keep you all straight. He's the king of cryptic assholes, though, popping in at random times to tell me I need to 'become' and dishing out some epic pain."

A rusty sounding laugh escaped from Titan seeming to take him by surprise. "Cryptic asshole. Yes. I will have to remember that. Has he said anything else of import?"

I ignored his questions. It was my turn to get answers. "How did you get here, Titan? Weren't you a statue in Bennett's courtyard last time we chatted?"

"You call this teleporting, I believe." Titan walked closer, and I noticed he had finally opted to cover himself in a long black kilt. "My powers are now growing, as are yours. You have found the second Chosen, and she has awakened my sister. Gaia's gifts are now yours as well."

"I don't want—"

His hand brushed my cheek freezing the rain upon my skin. "Power comes not to those that seek it but to those who can wield it. You are pure of heart. Yet all hearts can be blackened. Do not let your pain and fear turn you from the light."

"Alone ..."

"Yes, the path you walk is yours alone to carve. It can be a brutal and lonely journey. Yet it does not have to be a burden for one." The vines tightened around me as if offering comfort. The rain turned warm, tasting of salty tears on my lips and thawing the ice on my cheek. "Do not make the same mistakes as I did. Light and dark. The two sides exist because they must." He stepped back and opened his arms. The rain and vines disappeared. My clothes dried and an iridescent hooded cloak wrapped around my shoulders. "A gift for the Chosen. Keep it close, it may prove useful."

Grayson appeared by my side and immediately put himself between me and Titan. "My lady, stay behind me."

Titan studied the young boy with a bemused expression. "I admire your bravery, young Themis. I do not wish your Adelfi harm. Guard her well for she has need of you."

Then he disappeared.

Grayson turned, checking me over for injuries and let out a relieved sigh. "I heard your scream but was too late to reach you before you teleported. What happened, my lady?"

"I was beamed up by the God of Chaos and brought here," I replied, rubbing my tingling back. "Where am I?"

"You are still in Prometheus, my lady," he reassured me. "This is the temple at the peak of the mountain where the people come to pray to and speak with the God of Chaos."

"Why is—"

"Look out!" Grayson shouted and grabbed my shoulders spinning us around.

I stumbled backward and screamed as a sword pierced through Grayson's chest. Blood soaked his gray T-shirt and bubbled from his lips exactly like I had seen in my dream. Grayson's lips moved silently, telling me to run. Over his shoulder Guide Christos Athan grimaced and pulled his sword free. Terror held me hostage as I watched my friend fall to his knees, his hands pressed to the hole near his heart as blood seeped between his fingers.

"I would have spared you, boy, but you had to jump in the way." Christos said, looking genuinely regretful about having run Grayson through. "May the God of Chaos speed your soul through the judgment of the underworld and grant you life eternal in the stars."

I fought my way out of the paralyzing grip of terror and made my shaky limbs obey me as I angled my way over to Grayson. Christos's sword followed my every move. "Please let me see if I can help him."

My powers stirred, reaching out for Grayson as I got closer. Bennett had once told me that there were some people in the House of Light that could heal others, but I had never healed anyone except myself before. I mentally sent out a desperate prayer hoping someone was listening: *Gods, please don't let Grayson die. Guide my powers so that I can heal him.* Just as I was in reach of Grayson, the sword slashed down between us making me jump back. "Why are you doing this?" I shouted in anguish.

"Why am I doing this?" Christos repeated my question and looked at me like it should be obvious. "Because you don't deserve what you have taken: the throne or your intended bond-mate." He took a menacing step forward, and I stepped back. His dark eyes reflected his staunch belief in every word he spoke. "You are the pestilence that is plaguing my House. You bring your human rules here and disrespect our traditions. You dishonor the great Kyrion Calidora and tempt her son into believing you are his true bond-mate. I heard Kyrion Calidora myself when she picked my daughter as Kyrion Bennett's intended bond-mate when they were no more than seven." He punctuated each accusation with a thrust of his sword. "Never before have the Olympians attacked our watch towers until you came. Never before has the Moirai faltered. You will bring only death and destruction to my people."

"You don't have to do this. We can make a FailArmy video later all about my screwups and forget this ever happened," I begged, my knees feeling like jelly as I dodged that sharp blade and tried to get around him.

"Raise your sword, imposter. Let us put an end to your influence before you weaken my House further."

"I don't want to fight you. Please, let me help Grayson." Fear and anguish fed my powers, green and red flares arced from the glowing ball of light at my center looking for a way out.

"Better he dies with you than be forced to live with the disgrace of his failure to fulfill his oath when you die." Christos swung the sword, missing me by inches as I ducked. "Call your sword. I will make your death quick out of respect for Kyrion Bennett."

"I don't know how to call the sword!" I stumbled and almost fell. "I'm not your enemy. Please don't do this."

"So be it," Christos declared, as he took a firm grip on his sword clearly done toying with me. "I can't allow you to live and continue this hold you have over the Kyrion and the fate of my people. I'm sorry."

"Sorry! Really? Me too, about a bunch of things, but I'm not trying to kill anyone over it." A volcano of darkness tried to erupt from under the solid portion of my lonely highway, but I blocked it out. No way was I going down without a fight. Grayson needed me. I had relationships to mend with Dia, Molly, and Bennett before I died. Bennett—gods, this would break his heart when he found out one of his own people had betrayed him. "I'm already bonded to Bennett, you fucktard! If you kill me, you kill him too."

Christos paused for a moment, but then shook his head. "You lie. Kyrion Bennett is a good, honorable leader he would never disregard the bonding traditions. No, I will cut you out of our lives like the rotten limb that you are, and the Kyrion will bond with Selene as was meant."

I side-stepped to the right as the blade cut through the air and a line of pain scorched across my stomach. I pivoted left as another blow came at me and the sword sliced a line along my thigh. "Fuck this," I snarled and unleashed my powers. A tree branch shot from my palm, its limbs alight with fire as it hurtled forward to pierce his chest. Christos pivoted and brought his sword down, cutting off the branch. My other hand lifted shooting a fireball that caught him in the shoulder and threw him off balance. He came back at me full force, and I belatedly remembered my armor. I willed the necklace to shield me barely managing to cover one arm in time to prevent him from hacking it off. It caught him by surprise, and I managed to get a kick past his guard, making him stumble back and giving me some breathing room.

Movement caught my attention as Grayson fell to his side onto the ground, his face gray with blood loss. I cried out. "Grayson, hold on!" But he lay still and didn't answer.

My concentration wavered and my armor dissolved. Panic took over and a wave of power erupted from me. A choked scream tore from my throat, "You killed him!"

The next thing I knew I was standing over Christos Athan, and the sword I had purchased from Mark was in my hand, its black blade buried in the older man's chest. Red tendrils of power swirled up from his body and were sucked into the sword. Blue flames lit within the blade for a moment before it went dark once more. I released my grip on the hilt and dropped to my knees beside the man. Despair filled me. This time the death staining my hands was as real as the blood I uselessly tried to keep from spilling out around the sword.

"The Achlys," Christos choked out in a raspy whisper. "The god-killer sword has not been seen since the days of the gods." His eyes were wide with pain and wonder. "It is true, you *are* the Chosen of the God of Chaos. Forgive me,

Chosen. I am sorry for trying to scare you away and for attacking you."

My heart ached painfully for my dead friend but I had to know why all of this had happened. "That time on the basement stairs when it got really hot, that was you?"

"Yes," he admitted, tears welling in his dying eyes. "I heard from the servants that you had angered the Kyrion and made him snap at them. I wanted you to leave before he fell further under your influence."

"We were training, and things got a bit out of hand," I explained vaguely, not wanted to dredge up what Bennett had put me through that day. "The note to send out the runners to Paris and the attack at the pool, was that you too?"

The guide's brow knitted in confusion. "But you wrote the note? What attack?"

I stared at him. If neither of those had been Christos, who else was out to see me removed from the House of Chaos?

"Never mind," I replied. "What I want to know is why you decided I had to die?"

His breath wheezed for a moment, and he coughed up more blood.

"My daughter, Selene, is a strong and dutiful woman. She has fought hard to get where she is today. I only wanted what was best for her and my people." He grimaced as the coughing shifted the sword, and I reached to pull it free. His bloody hand grasped mine, clasping it with the sword to his punctured chest.

"No, my lady. If you pull the sword out the blood will flow free, and I will not be able to say what I need to. Today, when you damaged Kyrion Calidora's painting, my daughter cried for the first time since the day our lady died. I could not stand to see my little girl in pain. I overheard a part of your argument with Kyrion Bennett in the conference room and saw that you are his weakness. I could not let you continue to hurt either of them.

"I have dishonored my daughter and betrayed my Kyrion with my actions." Pain dug harsh lines across his brow as if his actions hurt worse than the sword buried in his chest. "I do not ask for me, but my daughter's sake. I beg that you spare her the burden of my mistakes." He gripped my hand tightly until I nodded, and the tension left his body. "I'm sorry, my lady. My daughter was wrong to try to force you into the likeness of Kyrion Calidora. Just as I was wrong. I let a father's and soldier's fears drive me to this disgrace."

"Shhh. Save your strength," I pulled at the rip in my shirt and pressed the torn cloth around his wound. My lonely highway trembled deep inside me as images of another man lying dead because of me and the body of my friend lying only feet away tried to overwhelm me. I pushed it back down and focused on the here and now.

"W-would you let me tell you my story, my lady?" Christos swallowed thickly, his eyes filling with tears. "Maybe someday you can find it in your heart to tell my daughter."

"Stay with me, Christos, so you can tell her yourself," I pleaded and mentally called out to Selene.

"It's too late for me, my lady," he gave me a tired smile. "Please."

"Tell me your story," I said, swallowing thickly as tears slipped down my cheeks. We had both lost enough today. "I'll make sure your daughter knows it."

His fingers trembled with his failing strength as he unzipped his chest pocket, pulling out a photo and a black medallion in the shape of the House of Chaos symbol and thrust them into my hand. "I met the love of my life the year after I finished my guide training," he began with a wistful smile. "I was selected as guide for our House during the Games that year. Back then there were many spectators for the Games. Great feasts were had, and all manner of ceremonies took place, even bonds. My love was the only daughter of a powerful family there to complete the Bonding Ceremony with a man she had been promised to. We knew as soon as we saw each other that our bond was true, but her father would have never let her become the bond-mate of a guide with weaker powers than her own. We met in secret as often as we dared right up to the day of her bond ceremony.

"It broke my heart to see her claimed by another, but what could we do? She would never have survived life as an outcast," he coughed, and blood flecked his beard. "I didn't know she carried my child until she showed up at my station one day nearly five months later. Her family had disowned her. Kyrion Calidora heard our conversation and took her in. We were to be bonded, but she died giving birth to our daughter." A single tear slipped from the corner of his eye as he turned his head toward me. Regret and longing were laid bare on his face. "I was too caught up in my own mourning to be a father. By the time I realized my error it was too late, and my daughter had become a strong, beautiful young woman. There is not a day that goes by that I do not regret never being there for her and telling her how much I have loved her." His hand tightened on mine once more. "Please, if there is any mercy you can spare, not for me, but for her, will you tell her that her father died an honorable death?"

Tears continued to slip down my cheeks, and I swallowed down the lump in my throat to say, "I'll tell her the truth. That you protected her and your people until your last breath."

His gaze returned to the sky and a surprised smile bloomed across his face. "Milli, my love. I've missed you."

His chest heaved a last ragged breath, and great wracking sobs shuddered through me. Was everyone around me destined to die? Was the future I saw in my dreams inevitable? No, I wouldn't let that happen: I would save the people I loved or die trying.

I folded Christos's hands across his chest. Then shoveled a hole in my lonely highway and tossed in the guilt and heartache to be taken out at a different time when I could deal with them. I stuffed the photo and medallion into my jeans pocket. Sobs continued to wrack me as I dragged myself across the ground to Grayson, pulling his still body into my arms and cradling him against my chest. Then I felt his heart beat faintly under my bloody fingertips. I gathered my powers once more and let them flow through me, but I didn't know how to direct them. Healing had never been a conscious thing for me—it happened automatically when I was injured. The red flares I saw inside me were my fire power and the green were—apparently—my earth power. What did my healing power look like?

I bowed my head and pressed my cheek again Grayson's. He was the only person who believed in me and stuck by me without fail. I couldn't lose him. His chest lifted on one final shuddering breath, then went silent. An anguished wail spilled from my lips as I rocked his limp body and smoothed back a lock of his unruly hair.

Gods, please help me save him. I will do anything that you ask. Please!

24

I pressed my palms to Grayson's lifeless chest and fire shot out around my hands burning away sections of his shirt. The fire died away and vines slithered from between my fingers to wrap around his torso. I angrily ripped the useless vines from him and tossed them aside. My right fist pounded against the stone floor, and I watched as my knuckles healed, but no light flared inside me that I could grab onto and force into Grayson. I couldn't find the source of my healing powers no matter what I tried.

"Bring him back. Do you hear me. You fucking gods can't have him." I wiped the tears from my face and tipped my head back to shout at the starry sky above. "Damn you, help me! I'll be the weapon in your war. I'll piece together the prophecy. I'll do whatever you want, just bring him back."

The familiar *thump-thump, whir, tickety-tock* sound of the Moirai filled the air. Then the God of Chaos's voice boomed, *"Remember what you have promised, creation."*

Warmth built along my spine and a golden light glowed around my hands where they rested on Grayson's chest. The warmth increased until I was sweating, and the light spread over his body, blinding me. My glowing ball of powers pulsed, growing larger. Then the world dropped away as we were teleported.

We landed in a meadow with Grayson still clutched tightly to my chest. The grass swayed around us, brushing along my arms and legs as if to comfort me. I recognized the training floor of Titan Tower, but something was different. The air felt oppressive and still, as if in anticipation of something. But my attention was captured by the faint rhythmic beat that was growing under my palms. I held my breath, barely daring to believe that the God of Chaos would bring Grayson back to me. Suddenly, his body jerked in my arms, and he gasped for breath. I closed my eyes sending thanks up to the heavens.

Grayson's eyes opened, and he looked up at me in confusion. "My lady, are you all right?"

I laughed feeling overwhelmed with relief and gratitude. Grayson gripped my hand in his as if he too needed that connection right now to reassure him that we were both alive.

"I'm fine," I said, my voice raspy from the tears and shouting. "How do you feel?"

I helped Grayson to sit up and the cut on my thigh protested the movement. The bloody gash looked deeper than I had realized and burned as my weakened powers slowly began the healing process. Grayson ran his hands over his chest, wiping away the blood to reveal only a faint white line where the sword had pierced him. "I feel ... amazing. How can that be? I remember the guide stabbing me and going after you, my lady."

"The important part is that we're still alive," I said, not wanting to talk about what happened with Christos or my deal with the devil—er, god, "but don't ever jump in front of a sword like that again."

"I cannot make that promise where you are concerned, my lady," Grayson said, sounding sorry for worrying me but determined to do it again if necessary.

Before I could lecture him, shouts rang out around us as someone noticed our presence. I called out for a doctor, wanting to make sure Grayson was really ok. A few minutes later a doctor appeared next to us. He checked Grayson over, declaring him healthy but recommending rest after I explained what had happened. My identity wasn't questioned here and within moments servants gathered around us clamoring to offer their assistance. I ordered Grayson to be taken to my old rooms on the contestants' floor to rest. Thankfully, the doctor was in agreement and the shot he gave Grayson knocked him out before he could protest too much.

I refused to be carted off and used my Kyrion-in-training status for the first time to order them all away. My powers were replenishing, and I was nearly all healed. I didn't need babysitters, I needed answers. Now that Grayson was safe, I could give my attention over to the growing feeling that something was wrong here. The servants had been very persistent about wanting me to leave this floor until I flat out refused. Why had the God of Chaos brought us here? What didn't the servants want me to see?

Tree limbs groaned and popped in the forest several feet to my left. Whispers echoed through my head that I somehow knew came from them. *The Goddess is woken. Dia has died. Gaia's warrior Kòri is born. Dia is Chosen. Dia is Kòri. Dia is born. Dia. Dia. Dia.* I envisioned a door in my mind and slammed it shut, locking out the cacophony of whispers. Three words they had said echoed through my mind.

Dread pooled in my stomach as I frantically climbed to my feet under the sheer force of adrenaline. I had watched one person die today, and another be brought back from the dead. The pavement of my lonely highway strained with the pressure of the nightmares seeking to escape, and if anything had happened to Dia it would break wide open.

I started toward the elevators but stopped when I noticed a gathering near the lagoon. Not more than fifty yards away the six guides representing each House in the Games formed a wall around the lagoon area. Beyond them I could see the Kyrion, Dia's grandmother, and another woman gathered around some kind of large egg-shaped rock. My heart beat heavily against my ribs as I approached the area not knowing what I would find but some sense telling me it wasn't going to be good. The line of guides refused to allow me through, so I teleported to the other side slamming into a solid wall of muscle. Bennett gripped my arms, keeping me from darting around him.

"Lia, my gods, what happened to you?" Bennett brought my hands up between us and flecks of dried blood sloughed off. I couldn't focus on the blood on my hands or it would pull me down into the pit of nightmares under my lonely highway.

"I'm fine," I replied absently, as I peered around his shoulder. Jaxon leaned over the egg-like rock, caressing its surface. His hair was a mess, his usually spotless clothes were ripped and dirt-smeared. "Where's Dia?"

"Were you attacked? Is this your blood?" Bennett gripped my shoulders trying to get my attention, but my senses were tingling telling me Dia was in trouble. That fickle-ass god wouldn't make me trade one friend's life for another, would he?

I called Dia's name and asked where she was, but no one

would answer me. I should have stayed. I shouldn't have let Bennett take me away no matter how mad Dia had been. I should have made her talk to me and stayed to work this out. *Oh gods, please don't let her be dead.* I would give up everything to keep my best friend safe. My powers grew as fear ate at me. Someone shouted that the meadow was growing taller and the trees were swaying restlessly. Fire ignited around my hands.

"Lia, you need to remain calm." Bennett cupped my cheeks forcing my eyes up to his and ran his fingers through my now mostly shoulder-length hair to grip it at the base of my neck. "Look at me. Focus. I will tell you what we know, but you have to calm yourself."

I swallowed down the fear that wanted to overtake me and took a shaky breath. "This is me being calm. Now, tell me what's happened to Dia."

He held me a moment longer, a flash of something that looked a lot like pain and longing darkening his eyes before the shields came down. "Jaxon and Dia have become bond-mates. He was tracking her progress in the competition through their connection. She won by finding the true entrance to Pètra Skià Kàstro—Stone Shadow Castle. But she opened a portal in one of the monoliths and fell through."

My breath sucked between my teeth, and I gripped Bennett's button-up shirt. Inarticulate sounds spilled from my lips as I tried to draw breath around the terror lodged in my throat. His hands grasped mine. "As best Jaxon can tell, she fell into the underworld and woke Gaia. After that, their connection cut off. All we know is that Dia used Jaxon's Kyrion name—Eros—to call him to her. He teleported to Shadow Ridge where the castle sits and found the other contestants gathered around that egg-shaped boulder of lava rock." Bennett nodded his head to the rock Jaxon was whispering to near the edge of the lagoon. "Jaxon has not been able to feel Dia through their connection but one of the contestants swore he saw her curled inside the rock."

I rested my head against Bennett's chest taking comfort from his nearness. His fingers brushed gently along my cheek, but he didn't hug me to him or kiss my head. Then everything that had happened between us earlier hit me, and I pushed away from him.

"I want to see her," I demanded.

"The rock is solid and has withstood all attempts to break the surface. We cannot use heavy equipment for fear of hurting Dia. There is nothing you can do." The ruthless leader of the Paldimori stared down at me from the face of the man I loved. "The Kyrion are deliberating over other alternatives. You will wait here until we give you permission to approach the rock."

An uncomfortable silence fell over the Kyrion, who had been close enough to hear his order.

"Damn you, Bennett. Don't pull that Kyrion bullshit with me. This is Dia we're talking about, my best friend—my sister." Green and red lights lit up my core reacting to my anger. My powers twined together even stronger than they had been before. They clamored to ride the wave of the jumbled ball of emotions building in me.

"Regardless, you will obey my orders," Bennett said in a cold voice.

"Let me through," I demanded, standing my ground. My voice cracked as I confessed, "I *need* to see Dia."

For a split second his frosty look thawed, and I thought he would relent. "Stop," Selene's command split through the tense silence like a whip. She teleported across the area to stand by Bennett. The composed shell of the Diplomatic

Doll had cracked revealing raw pain and a searing loathing entirely directed at me. I gulped at Selene's white-knuckled grip on the sword at her hip, expecting her to behead me at any moment. The tension mounted as she communicated telepathically with Bennett, never moving her eyes off me.

Bennett took in my ripped shirt and bloody body. His face was pale as he insisted, "Tell me what happened at the temple."

My throat locked up around the words. I looked down at my blood-stained hands seeing Christos's face as he breathed his last breath. In my mind he morphed into the man from my time on the streets, those lifeless blue eyes accusing me as his blood dripped from the knife in my hand. My breath hitched when the scene in my head changed to the fork in the road on my lonely highway. The swirling wall of mists to my left turned darker and inky black tendrils spread across the landscape, leaving in its wake dozens of bodies. Bennett lying in a pool of blood. Molly crushed beneath a fallen wall. On and on it went. It shook me so badly that it took me a moment to realize Selene was talking.

"... ran her sword through Guide Christos Athan's chest," Selene accused.

"It was an accident!" I shouted, shoving my way free of the images that filled my mind like a horror show.

"As the desecration of Kyrion Calidora's painting was an accident?" Selena asked with bitter disdain.

Several of the other Kyrion mumbled in outrage. A shield popped up around us like Jaxon had used at the police station to keep others from overhearing us. I could see it now, extending out around the three of us like a snow globe. The other Kyrion stood outside of our bubble watching with various reactions: Nyx and Tartarus seemed disappointed to be missing the drama, Erebus was quiet and watchful as always, while Gaia pursed her lips in typical disapproval where I was concerned. Jaxon was still trying to release Dia from the rock.

Hold on Dia, I'm coming for you.

"I shouldn't have lost my temper and damaged your mother's painting," I admitted. "But I didn't mean to kill Christos." Thinking quickly, I made up the most believable lie that wouldn't incriminate either of us. "There was a fight. One of the Omàda must have slipped into the city. It was dark and when I turned, he was just there." I blocked out the feeling of the sword in my hand as I stood over the dying man. "Christos died trying to protect his people. Please you've got to believe me. I would never—"

"What should we believe, Lia? That you—who can barely control your powers or defend yourself— 'accidentally' killed one of our oldest and most skilled guides?"

"I'm so sorry." I choked down the tears clogging my throat and swallowed thickly against the sick feeling churning in my stomach. "Trust me, I know it sou—"

"Trust," Bennett scoffed, "We seem to keep coming back to that point."

"Like you've been the poster boy for trust?" I said sarcastically. Everything I had been holding back since setting foot in Prometheus came flying out of my mouth. "You brought me to your home without any warning that I was going to be put through Kyrion boot camp and forced into becoming just like your mother. You turned back into the asshat I first met and tormented me with my most painful memories during training. How could you do that to me?"

Selene pushed in front of Bennett. "You have no idea what he has done for you," she stated, her cheeks flushed with anger. "Bennett is the only reason you aren't still in a jail cell and your precious art gallery being sold off piece-by-piece to pay off your loan."

"Sele—," Bennett tried to interrupt, but she was on a roll.

"Bennett may have used his power and influence to help ruin you, but he has more than made up for it." Selene's hands balled into fists as if it was taking all of her willpower to keep from punching me. "Yet, you are still punishing him."

My shocked gaze met Bennett's, and I felt the blood drain from my face. That haunted and guilty look I had been seeing on his face more recently confirmed everything. The police had never been able to find evidence that Natalie had been behind the embezzlement part of my charges. The harassing phone calls to local artists and the supposed additional bill of lading fees added when I shipped art to other galleries, that would take someone with a lot more connections than Natalie to pull off.

"It was you that framed me for embezzlement." Pain ripped through me at Bennett's betrayal.

Selene turned to Bennett, the anger bleeding away into a contrite look as she realized what she had done. "I'm sorry, Bear. That wasn't my truth to tell."

The tic in Bennett's jaw beat madly as he watched me intently as if trying to read my thoughts even though our connection was closed. "No, Selene, do not apologize for saying what needed to be said."

My voice was no more than an anguished whisper when I asked, "Why?"

Bennett reached out for me, but I stepped back, sure if he touched me I would break apart. He dropped his hand, those dark eyes full of misery that I tried to ignore. "I have protected Natalie and Jaxon since my mother defied our laws and welcomed in refugees from another House. Nat was my little sister. She was mine to protect. When she came to me about the monster abusing her and the inept human laws that did nothing, I wanted to kill you. It was Nat that spared your life and convinced me you needed to suffer." He grimaced. "Jaxon was right. I should have checked my source to determine the truth for myself."

My trembling hands gripped my elbows as I tried to hold the shredded pieces of myself together. All this time, and he never said a thing. "Would you have ever told me?"

"I do not know." Regret was stamped into the haggard lines of his face as he ran his fingers through his spiky hair. "I have made many decisions as Kyrion and have never looked back. Yet, I question myself constantly when it comes to you. Did I feel guilt and remorse for my actions? Yes. I have almost told you a million times before now, but I had too many sins to atone for already. If I had told you this that day we talked while sitting in the yard behind your condo, would you have ever given me another chance?" Bennett asked quietly. I stared at him while the tears slipped silently down my cheeks, unable to answer. He nodded. "That is what I thought."

Selene made a strangled noise of frustration, "Bennett has suffered for what he did to you and has more than made up for his mistakes. He sent Jaxon to investigate the accusations against you and got you out of jail. Then he bought that pitiful excuse for a bank in your human town to keep you from losing your business. You've been given the luxuries of a Kyrion"—her expression said that they were clearly not deserved—"without taking on a fraction of the duties because he didn't want to overburden you. And you have no idea what our people are suffering at the hands of our enemies while you insult the greatest woman I have ever known. The only parent I have ever known," she finished in a lost-little-girl voice.

Bennett had bought the bank to pay off my business loan saving me from losing my gallery. Why had he kept all of this from me? Was there no end to the secrets he kept? Everything we had built together crumbled before me. I couldn't bear to look at him and turned my attention to Selene.

"You clearly loved Calidora deeply. I'm sorry that she's gone, but I can't be her. Don't set me on a pedestal because I'm doomed to fall off and disappoint you." My gaze finally landed back on Bennett and it was like the air was sucked from the room. "I've tried so hard, but the lies—"

A loud agonizing sob issued from my throat. My lonely highway erupted with a burst of visions and feelings that threatened to overwhelm me. I walked into the eye of the hurricane raging inside me and images from my past fluttered through my mind—pieces ripped from my blood-stained life. Pale, lifeless blue eyes of the man I had killed on the streets stared up at me. Christos's blood-splattered face cringed in agony. A hooded figure pressed me down onto a dirty mattress and tore at my clothes while I fought to get away. My father was pulled over the side of the boat to his death. The images poured into me—some real and some I had never experienced before—all threatening to drag me down into that dark place of despair that had led to the construction of my highway in the first place.

Never again.

Instead of trying to contain the storm, I let it rage. My power built until the concealing bubble around us burst, making my ears pop. My powers surged forward so quickly I didn't have time to stop the ball of fire that ripped from my chest, like all of the heartache had taken form. What looked like a burning ball of seaweed hit Bennett directly in the chest burning a large hole in his shirt. A ring of trees broke through the ground, imprisoning him in their circle. Burning boulders pushed up around him creating another circle to his cage. The water in the lagoon started to churn, creating waves that slapped against the shore. Vines grew from my palms and slithered through the boulders and trees creating a tightly woven web over Bennett.

For once I wasn't trying to deny my powers or snuff them out. Finally, it was like a couple of pieces of me clicked into place. It felt *good*.

I teleported over to the egg-like rock as shouts rang out behind me. Hopefully it would take a while for them to dig Bennett out and buy me some time to help Dia. Dia's grandmother stepped in front of me, blocking my way. Desperation to see my best friend alive rode me hard. I ignored the old woman and tested my newly formed earth powers on the rock. Nothing happened. "That's it, I'm roasting this thing."

"You will do no such thing, young lady." Dia's grandmother, Elder Rosella, elbowed me back. "The servants are still cleaning up the mess you made of your bond-mate."

I glanced behind me where Selene was hacking at the vines with her sword and busting through the rocks with balls of fire. Servants were sweeping up the debris as soon as it gathered on the ground. My control had slipped its leash, and this was the result. An apology was poised on the tip of my tongue, but I pressed my lips together locking it in. No, this was Bennett's fault.

"He deserved it," I snarled.

"Men usually do," Elder Rosella huffed, "but you cannot set fire to everything that gets in your way."

"Oh, I definitely can," I said as fire played over my

knuckles. "My best friend is stuck inside this lava rock like some deranged chicken. We're getting her out. Now step aside."

The old woman narrowed her faded blue eyes. Her dark skin creased even more with the scowl she aimed my way. The metal discs and beads woven into her white braids vibrated, sounding like a rattlesnake. Words spilled from her mouth in a language I didn't understand. Then she switched to English. "Insolent. Rash. Disrespectful—"

"Give it a rest Prune-Elda." I dodged to her left but winced in pain when her cane rapped against my shin. "Motherfucker! That hurt."

"What language." A satisfied grin spread across her wrinkled lips before she hid it behind a disapproving look. "My granddaughter should have better taste in friends."

Before I could respond, shards of rock flew through the air. Over the top of Elder Rosella's head, I could see a slender but well-muscled arm had punched through the lava rock. Then the rock melted away revealing an unfamiliar naked woman. She floated up from the remains of the egg and dropped to the floor in a crouch. If it weren't for the vivid blue eyes that I knew so well, I would never have guessed the woman sporting buns and abs of steel was Dia. What had the gods done to her?

I gasped, "Good god, she's like the Terminator."

I rushed to Dia's side, taking in the three symbols on her back with anger. Dia stood up, and I could tell she was several inches taller than she had been before. I took off the robe that Titan had given me and wrapped it around her naked body. It turned a green color with little swirls of lotus flowers. Dia seemed to be in a daze, but when Jaxon nudged me aside to kiss her, I realized they must have been talking telepathically. Jaxon bundled up his bond-mate and carted her off before I could do more than whisper an apology and promise we would talk later.

I turned to find myself facing one extremely pissed off bond-mate and a line of grim-faced Kyrion. "Do not move," Bennett stated. The air around us vibrated with the power of his command, and I found myself unable to move.

"Bennett, let me go. I need time to figure out where we go from here. You can't force me to talk to you," I stated, still feeling raw from everything I had learned today. "I've never pledged myself to a House. You aren't *my* Kyrion. Now release me."

"You changed the outcast law. You are living in Prometheus at the moment, which makes you a refugee in my House. You may be Chosen and my bond-mate, but you are not beyond my rule," Bennett gritted out, every harsh word a lash against my already battered heart. "I have been far too lenient with you. Did my Archai not warn you that if you disobeyed me—if you violated our laws—you would be punished? You killed a member of your House and openly attacked your Kyrion."

"I already told you Christos's death was an accident. Why won't you believe me?" This wasn't Bennett trying to force me to talk to him so we could try to mend everything broken between us. A feeling of apprehension stirred as the other five Kyrion stood shoulder to shoulder, presenting a united front. "I kicked your ass for being a manipulative prick. What are you accusing me of?"

"Jillian Nova Davies, refugee of the House of Chaos, you are accused of the murder of Guide Christos Athan and treason against your Kyrion," Bennett declared. His voice in my head was like an ice shard driving into me as he said, "*I warned you that there are repercussions for every action we take. You made your choices, and now I am forced to make mine.*"

Bennett's door to our connection closed with a click that reverberated through me like a shotgun blast. In all these months he had never once closed the door on his side. It felt as if he had taken all the warmth with him, and I wrapped my arms around myself trying to generate some heat. I was truly alone now. The lump in my throat grew to a boulder that no more words would fit past. I nodded and dug my nails into my palms to keep the tears at bay. Here was everything I had feared. That the Bennett I had come to love was the lie, and the cold and ruthless Kyrion I had first met all those months ago was the real man under all those complex layers.

I couldn't move if I tried as Selene came forward and slipped the kóvo cuff over my bicep.

"Come," she said, her voice filled with hate and triumph. "You will stand trial for your crimes, prisoner."

LEAVE A REVIEW

Thanks so much for giving my book a try!

I hope that you enjoyed the story. If so, it would be super awesome if you could share this book
on **Facebook** and **Twitter**. And even more amazing if you could leave your feedback for me and others by posting a review on **Amazon** and/or **Goodreads**.

Your feedback and support go a long way in helping new authors like me.

Happy reading,
T.L. Callahan

ACKNOWLEDGMENTS

Thanks so much to my street team, the Dragon's Hoard, who always provide great feedback and support. Thanks to my family who puts up with my very late writing nights, my daydreaming about characters, and my vampire-like allergy to mornings. Extra special thank you to my editor, Bernadette, who has helped me to grow so much as a writer. My stories wouldn't be nearly as well-told without you!

Thank you so much to you, the readers, for giving my book a try. You make this possible and keep me pushing forward. Your reviews, comments, and follows mean so much more than words could ever express.

ABOUT THE AUTHOR

T.L. Callahan is the author of the fantasy romance adventure series Paldimori Gods Rising. She has always been a book lover; devouring romance, fantasy, and poetry since she was a young girl growing up in Kentucky. Her love for the outdoors inspired hours of wandering the woods pretending to be on adventures discovering magical creatures and being the heroine of her own stories. That hasn't changed much these days. Never knowing what you can find around the next corner keeps her seeking out new adventures from backpacking in the Wind River Range of Wyoming to piloting a sailboat down the Tagus River in Portugal. T.L. lives in Ohio with her husband, son, and a cat that thinks he's a dog.